Praise for
The Corpse in the Trash Room

When a story opens with a wake for a dead hamster that produces a corpse of the human variety, you suspect you're in for a romp. And that's what Colette Tajemna provides in this witty story that is part farce and every bit a satisfying mystery. I laughed as I puzzled out this masterful whodunit.

—James H Lewis,
author of the Chief Novak series

Fans of Sarah Caudwell will especially enjoy this clever mystery with its academic setting and subtle wit.

—Carolyn Korsmeyer, author of *Little Follies: A Mystery at the Millennium*

Funny, and at times nostalgic, author Colette Tajemna balances the sociological examination of a generation and a time with a good, old-fashioned mystery worthy of Agatha Christie—suspect after suspect pinpointed and then cast aside as the students barrel toward a satisfying denouement, wisecracking along the way."

— Steven Mayfield, award winning author of *The Penny Mansions* and *Treasure of the Blue Whale*

[T]he story unfolds with the charm and humor of a Jane Austen novel, drawing you in deeper with every turn of the page. Prepare to be captivated as the truth behind this gripping mystery reveals itself in a twist you never saw coming."

—Roslyn Reid, author of *A Scandal at Crystalline* and *The Spiricom*

COLETTE TAJEMNA

The Corpse in the Trash Room

Archelaus

Washington, DC

Published by *Archelaus*

archelaus-cards.com

© 2024 by Karla Huebner

All rights reserved. Except as permitted under the U. S. Copyright Act of 1976, no part of this publication may be reproduced, stored in a retrieval system, distributed, or transmitted, in any form or by any means, without the prior written permission from the publisher or author.

This is a work of fiction. Names, characters, businesses, places, items, brands, events, incidents, and events are either the products of the author's imagination or were used fictitiously. Any resemblance to actual persons, living or dead, or actual events is purely coincidental.

Cover design by K. Huebner

ISBN: 978-1-961852-07-5 (paperback)
ISBN: 978-1-961852-10-5 (large print paperback)
ISBN: 978-1-961852-06-8 (ebook)

In memory of
KDR

PREFACE

I am, I regret to say, well on the road to becoming an old man, and consequently my university has given me a firm nudge to retire. It is not that I have grown senile, nor that students have ceased signing up for my courses, but we have fewer students these days than we did in past years, and I am expensive (among the History professors—certainly not compared to the Business professors or the football coaches). It was intimated to the Liberal Arts faculty in general that if the older professors did not retire, then the junior, more recently hired ones would be discarded. And so, not wishing our younger colleagues ill, many of us have accepted a (not very large or impressive) Retirement Incentive Package.

In clearing out some of my old files, I came upon an ancient manila folder that had apparently slipped between the neat modern forest-green hanging folders. This manila folder was somewhat bent and grubby, but it was thick with papers, the edges of which were even more bent and grubby than those of the folder itself. Curious what this relic might be doing lurking amid my relatively tidy folders of lesson plans and notes for my scholarly articles and books, I drew it forth, careful not to let any of its loose pages slide out the sides and back into the depths of the drawer. What could it be? The title on the top tab was not printed on an adhesive label, nor written in bold ink, but was scrawled in faint and smudgy pencil. I could not quite even make it out, given that I await, with some trepidation, removal of my cataracts. (I had thought surely I must be too young for cataracts, but alas the eye doctor assures me that even people in their fifties sometimes require cataract surgery!)

Taking the folder over to my desk, I opened it, and seeing the pica-sized Courier letters of my first typewriter, the ink faint due to my infrequent and parsimonious changing of the ribbon, I was immediately transported back to a most curious episode from my youth—specifically, from my undergraduate days. Eager to remind myself of a happier time (albeit one interrupted by a corpse), I began to read ...

1

Under normal circumstances, our Hall is really a delightful place to live. I don't mean to imply that it has no ups and downs, or that there is never tension between any of its members, but I think all of us would agree that a better Hall than ours would be hard to find. The Housing Coordinator has designated our wing as Quiet with preference given to upper-division students, but we are in no way one of those moribund Quiet Halls in which everyone gloomily studies and can only listen to music through headphones. No, our Hall has chosen to be a Quiet Hall purely in that we take our studying seriously. Apart from that, we indulge in as much noise and silliness as we can manage—of, I must say, our own particular kind. We do not go in for kegger parties, communal pot-smoking, weekends on acid, or disco dancing in the lounge; and though we often play with our food in the cafeteria, we are not of that contingent which routinely throws apple cores at every person who gets up on the stage to make an announcement. We have, however, painted luminous stars all over the ceiling; decorated the bathroom with signs stolen from various campus functions; and hauled much of the furniture out of the lounge into the Hall's telephone alcove so as to have a cozier place in which to drink. From time to time the "Gang of Four"—Holly, Carolyn, Tricia, and Pauline—will sit together on the floor painting their Art and Costume Design assignments to the sound of the Dead Kennedys or English folk music; at other times we will all gather in front of my room to blow soap bubbles and listen to the Rolling Stones or the Chipmunks' Christmas album.

Yes, on the whole we are a compatible group despite our diversity of majors—which, at the risk of sounding like a typical dance-floor conversation ("What's your major?" is the university equivalent of "What's your sign?"), I will say include Theater (Holly and Carolyn), Art (Tricia and Pauline), Environmental Studies (Malcolm), and (in Evan's case), a shifting array of formidable-sounding disciplines. I myself am a historian, and in the interests of accuracy I will state that our Hall is not so small as to consist of a mere seven students, but as a historian who also appreciates a well-constructed narrative, I have not tried to include those of our number who studied adamantly throughout the events of the day. Though they too are our close comrades in silliness, when one considers that they have done little or nothing to warrant inclusion in this tale, and that I do not wish to burden the reader with a plethora of names and descriptions at the very outset (precisely when these are least likely to be appreciated), as a chronicler wrestling with considerations of art versus accuracy, in this matter I must choose art.

In all other areas I hope that my companions will find me truthful; I have sacrificed almost my entire Spring Break to this labor, but after all that is of little consequence.

I digress. No matter how my hallmates may wish to pick over this narrative and argue over wording and interpretation, the larger public will wish me to get on with my story and reveal just what occurred. The larger public will wish to know that Holly, Carolyn, Tricia, and Pauline are attractive young women of nineteen or twenty years of age, that—

No, the public's desire to know our precise ages, looks, and thoughts will have to wait. We must have Events. We must have Action. And so to begin!

The disturbance in our hitherto carefree lives began, I believe, when Carolyn's hamster, Beast, was found dead in its Habitrail late one night.

Lest you should think that this is going to be a story about a dead hamster, I must hasten to assure you that it is not. However, the discovery of Beast lying dead in her Habitrail was to prove the starting point—for us, at least—of considerably more serious events. Admittedly, there was nothing suspicious about the animal's death, but the timing might be described as opportune.

Not that Carolyn looked at it that way; quite the opposite.

I had just given up my study of Voltaire for the night and was settling down to read my Tintin books—in French, of course—when I was distracted from this simple pleasure by an outbreak of hysterical screaming down the hall. It sounded like Holly or Carolyn, but—though they are somewhat hysterical by nature—this sounded unusual. I opened my door.

Holly stood, hands on hips, in the hallway just outside Carolyn's room. "Beast is dead!" she was exclaiming. "Get in here Keith, we need you," she added abruptly upon sighting me. I complied, though without undue speed.

I suppose I liked Beast as much as did anyone—in fact, there are photos extant on Carolyn's wall that show me standing in the bathroom watching Beast emerge from a toilet-paper tube—but Beast was not really the sort of pet one could be more than mildly fond of. She was tame enough, if by "tame" you meant lacking all fear of humans, but she was neither intelligent nor affectionate. It was rather fun letting her scuttle up and down your sleeve, but beyond that, her interest lay primarily in her more tiresome habits—for Beast typically awoke only after Carolyn had finally gone to bed (usually between midnight and four, depending on the proximity of finals), whereupon she would make a great deal of noise of the rattling and scuffling variety prior to escaping from the Habitrail and somehow going via the radiator pipes into other people's bedrooms. In fact, Holly was already explaining that, she and Carolyn having returned from a really tiresome rehearsal, she had tried to divert Carolyn by saying "Why don't you see if Beast is in her cage?" Carolyn had then discovered the hyperactive little rodent dead—or, as she put it, "There was the damned animal sitting there dead with her snout in a tunnel!"

Despite this rather callous description of her pet, Carolyn had immediately let loose with that great wailing and cursing and gnashing of teeth which had torn me away from my beloved Tintin book; now she was flinging herself recklessly at her bed.

"I knew the little monster was going to peg out on me one of these days," she kept howling, "but why did it have to be tonight?"

"Peg out?" said Holly, clearly intrigued by the phrase.

"You know," wailed Carolyn, "croaked, kicked the bucket, bit the dust, gone to join the choir invisible ..."

"Oh," said Holly, entranced. "Pegged out ..." she repeated ecstatically, "I've never heard that one before." Then, anxious as usual to display her abilities as Stage Manager, she demanded that Evan and I confirm the diagnosis. We were not much inclined towards the role of coroner, but with a quick nudge or two we hastily ascertained the creature to be deader than a doornail.

A small crowd had now gathered around Carolyn's door, and she left off screaming in favor of making crude jokes about what should be done with the body. In the hope of calming her, we poured her a hefty dose of tequila—the last in the bottle—and, lacking a suitable canopic jar, dumped Beast into an Instant Powdered Lemonade can that had formerly held pencils, brushes, and an ink-encrusted Rapidograph or two. Carolyn wished to save the Dear Departed for a more ceremonious interment, so when she had finished with both her more violent weeping and her most strikingly tasteless jokes, we all returned to our respective quarters.

The next evening being Saturday, and Holly and Carolyn being yet again depressed over their obnoxious rehearsals (I could have told them that the director was an irritating woman, but they had been filled with a naïve desire to Get Experience at all costs), we remarked upon the lack of Hall Tequila. Piling into Holly's unnecessarily small car, about six of us descended upon the liquor store where I, being a more mature sort with valid ID, purchased a large supply of tequila and the things needful to its use. Back at the Hall, we then set up a table, and declared the event a wake for Beast. We attempted to speak with suitably Irish accents, but this lasted only until Relief Proctor Sally chanced by.

"A wake!" she cried upon being told what we were doing, "What fun!"

We invited her to join us, and, though abstaining from spirituous refreshment, she settled herself on the couch and began to compose a funerary limerick. Before long, however, she had to be on her way to perform her customary rounds and check any disturbances that might arise to mar a pleasant Saturday night, so we thanked her for the limerick and bade her a jolly adieu. We did not, of course, bother to note the time.

Our conversations continued in their usual enjoyable but unmemorable way, until Holly, far gone in her cups as she so rapidly becomes, took it upon herself to prove that she could walk a straight line. This was a miserable failure, so she reminded us from the floor that it was really time to see Beast to her final resting place.

"Do you mean the dump?" I inquired.

"I thought we were going to bury her in the middle of the Quad tomorrow during the Spring Fair," protested Carolyn. "I stole some forks to dig with."

The university was undergoing an enrollment crisis largely attributable to the ending of the Baby Boom, and the Administration apparently believed that, demographics notwithstanding, enrollment could be boosted with the aid of a really lavish Spring Fair. Thus, according to the Chancellor's propaganda, the Quad would be crawling with high school students and their keepers, and we had been mildly inclined to show them that life at **our** college has nothing to do with football.

"The ground's too hard," objected Evan. "You'll never get anywhere with a fork. Put the hamster down the trash chute and anyone who went to Catholic school can mumble some Latin—if," he added with a disapproving eye upon Carolyn's limp and intoxicated form, "**if** you're still going through that religious phase."

Evan is always ready to trample any idea unless he thinks he can add to it, and I believe that he considers Holly and Carolyn to be regrettably undisciplined and licentious young women, but unfortunately he was right about the dirt in the Quad. Years of student feet have compacted the ground so that it would have taken a bulldozer to dig anything there, and who knew whether the high school students would pay much attention to a group of lunatics burying an Instant Lemonade can, anyway.

Holly rose to her feet with some assistance from the wall. "Here, Carolyn, you hold the coffin," she insisted, as though anyone else had expressed an interest in pallbearing. The two of them then began to sing a dirge, employing such phrases as "Now she is dead,/ She will meet her final bed," and "Once she was red,/ Now she always will be dead," but this caused them to giggle inordinately and thus the rest of us to poke at them as we progressed down the corridor.

The trash chutes in our building are, by a stroke of rare intelligence on the part of the architect, located in a sort of No Man's Land near the stairs and the long-distance pay phone, this being an uncarpeted and only occasionally mopped region between Halls where no one of any sense spends longer than necessary. The trash chute itself is thoughtfully (or not so thoughtfully, if one is carrying a heavy or unwieldy load) secreted in a closet with floor space sufficient for piles of newspaper and two garbage cans into which we are requested to place glass and aluminum recyclables.

We halted in front of the door; to our astonishment, a note was taped there stating "Full—Use North Chute."

"That's ridiculous," said Carolyn. "I've never heard of a full trash chute."

"Apparently now you have," I said, and turned to go north. However, as Evan and Malcolm and Pauline and Tricia and I turned to go north, Holly flung open the door.

"What on earth ..." she began to demand, in the voice of the hardened Stage Manager, when she broke off and instead yelled "Keith!"

I turned, and she added "Malcolm!" for good measure while Carolyn, holding the Instant Lemonade can and looking somewhat stupid, though I daresay only stupefied, was staring into the doorway.

Inside was a figure slumped atop the can reserved for recyclable glass.

2

"You'd better move out of the doorway," I said, employing what I hoped to be a suitable blend of stern kindness and reassuring bravado. Feeling absurdly like Sergeant Friday of **Dragnet,** I strode forward and took a closer look.

Unhappily, I recognized the occupant. It was Richard Gurney, one of the dorm preceptors, apparently passed out. He was the sort of person who always tries to ingratiate himself with others but who succeeds only in offending; he was perhaps best known for holding sherry parties to which only two or three people would come. I sighed. Why had he chosen to spend the night in the trash closet? And why did *we* have to be the ones to find him?

Meanwhile, Evan had entered the closet and taken Gurney's hand. "I think he's dead," he announced.

Our shock at this pronouncement was considerable. Gurney looked like a man sleeping off a binge. His fair hair hung over his downturned face in strings, and his pose was careless. Besides, he couldn't have been much past thirty, and was neither fat nor sickly. One does not expect to find dead people in college dormitories, whereas one does occasionally discover people in strange and compromising situations. The idea of Richard Gurney sleeping something off in an awkward place was mildly annoying; the idea of Richard Gurney being dead was thoroughly unsettling. We recoiled as one from the open door.

"Oh-my-God," exclaimed Tricia, backing hastily away. Pauline began to laugh most unpleasantly, as she sometimes does when she thinks an injection of malice necessary, and Carolyn remarked "It figures!"

"What figures?" said Holly.

"That **we** would have to find him," replied Carolyn darkly.

This set Pauline off into further laughter, which Tricia attempted to quell by saying "Pauline, be quiet! My God, this is awful. What are we going to do? Are you sure he's dead, Evan?"

"He probably just passed out," said Holly. A thought appeared to strike her, and she turned to Evan with great displeasure. "You're just making it up to scare us! Evan Reid, I'm sick and tired of your stupid tricks, and I think that this one is really inappropriate."

Apparently she felt that a person who had once dressed as the Devil for Halloween was liable to play unusually cruel jokes upon his friends; however, Evan responded with commendable politeness. Looking rather grieved, he said "I assure you, Holly, that I am not that sort of person. Go and look at him yourself if you have any doubt in the matter."

Holly declined, and instead demanded that if Gurney were really dead, we must shut the door immediately as she did not think she could bear to look at him any longer.

"Close it right away," she exclaimed, "please, Keith, it's just too awful."

"Richard Gurney dead," said Tricia, "I can't believe it. I saw him at lunch today eating fish sticks."

"Well, there you have it," said Malcolm. "Stay away from the fish sticks."

Tricia replied that even under normal circumstances she would not be caught eating them, as they were always soggy.

"He's gone and croaked just to make life miserable for us," muttered Carolyn.

"Your regard for the deceased is most touching," said Evan. "I suppose you think we should tip him into the trash along with your hamster."

"That's about what he deserves," said Carolyn.

"What I'd like to know," said Malcolm mildly, "is how he ended up here in the first place."

I silently applauded Malcolm. He may not say much, but he has a firmer and more sensible grasp of reality than some people I could name. "You're absolutely right," I said. "Gurney has no business sitting on trashcans, dead **or** alive. In fact, it's not a place where anyone would want to sit, especially when feeling ill or queasy, so did he come there of his own accord or **was he placed there?**"

No one responded to this immediately; then Tricia, looking decidedly pale, said "Oh my God Keith, do you think somebody killed him?"

A degree of chaos broke out at this point. Both Pauline and Carolyn began to laugh, Pauline with the aforementioned malicious glee and Carolyn quite hysterically; Holly briefly abandoned the persona of Stage Manager and repeated "This is awful. Just awful," several times before she came to and grabbed Carolyn and shouted "Stop that! Stop it at once!" which to my surprise had the desired effect. She then sat Carolyn, who was still clutching the Instant Lemonade can, on the floor, whereupon Malcolm said, in his quiet, rational way, "Don't you think we should do something about this?"

"Yes, of course," I said, wishing I had thought to bring this up first myself.

"Oh God, I wish I had just gone to bed or at least finished my drawings for Louise's class," said Tricia. "I've never seen a body before."

"You haven't seen a **dead** body before, you mean," said Holly. "Don't forget that model in Life Drawing!"

"Back to the subject at hand ..." I said hastily. I did not feel it necessary that they go off on the distasteful and pointless subject of the Model from Life Drawing, whose reputed resemblance to me had been such that a study of him embellished with my name had been taped to my door. Besides, the Model from Life Drawing had been unquestionably nude, while Richard Gurney was clothed in his usual jeans and chambray shirt.

"Well—" said Holly, and the discussion was on. The more civic-minded of our number were in favor of calling the police or perhaps the Health Center, while certain others seemed to feel that the deceased deserved to spend the night on a trash can. I pointed out that, whether or not Gurney deserved to spend the night in the trash, wandering freshmen on acid ought not to run across him and require psychiatric care. Evan, to be sure, felt that any freshman wandering the building on acid was asking for trouble; Holly objected that it had already given **us** a bad trip and that no one on acid thinks to take out the trash anyway.

Throughout this discussion, Carolyn sat on the floor glaring and badmouthing the deceased, and making such remarks as "First the hamster and now that pervert Gurney, it's enough to make me lose my brain and my dinner all at once. Fuck this shit, I want to die," which caused Evan to glance reprovingly in her direction.

However, at last we agreed to call the campus police; we did not feel it necessary to subject Relief Proctor Sally to the vileness of Richard Gurney in corpse-form, especially after she had been so kind as to write Beast's funerary limerick.

I shall pass over the arrival of the police and their subsequent tests, measurements, and questions. Had they permitted us to view them in action, it would have been different, but we were almost immediately hustled off to our lounge to be questioned by officers Denny and Morales, a businesslike pair whose actions were surprisingly dull to observe and would be more so to relate. Officer Denny, a large fellow in his mid-fifties, was perhaps most notable for being the first Black person I had observed to possess dark palms, an irrelevant fact as startling to me as my original discovery at the age of seven or eight (made while standing shivering in line on the edge of the pool at the local Y) that Joey Patterson's were pink. As for Officer Morales, he lacked even so minor a distinguishing trait, unless it was his comparative silence during the interview process.

And once officers Denny and Morales had ascertained that we all recognized the corpse and that not only did we appear to possess a mutual alibi but that we had noticed nothing unusual during the course of the evening, their interest in us evaporated. We did at last overhear that the cause of death looked likely to have been a blow to the neck resulting in laryngeal trauma, but they refused to tell us anything whatsoever, thus frustrating us in our natural thirst for knowledge. Altogether, we were much disappointed.

However, their lack of interest in us had its reassuring side. It would not have been pleasant to have been suspected of murdering Richard Gurney, and when I considered the sullen and foul mood evinced by Carolyn, I found it somewhat remarkable that the police had not detained her for questioning. She had persisted in the senseless notion that Gurney had died purely to trouble us, repeating such remarks as "He was a fucking pain in the ass," until she at last got up, saying "Pardon me, I'm going to vomit."

Tricia took one look at her, said "Gosh, Carolyn, you look awfully pale. I better go with you," and, taking her arm, propelled her to the bathroom. All of this probably planted Carolyn firmly in the minds of the police as a belligerent drunk; luckily there was no way for them to know that this was not normally her way.

For Carolyn, though she will not often turn down a drink, and though she is perhaps overly fond of vigorous language, is fundamentally a decent sort (even if Evan does consider certain of her wall decorations to be quite **in**decent), and she is not at all given to violence (even if she has told Malcolm that she wished to hurl Evan from the third-floor balcony). She spends most of her time rehearsing plays and studying medieval French, and the notepad on her door is typically covered with the likes of "You're needed at the Costume Room tomorrow—call them if it's not possible," "Cheryl wants to know when you will be at rehearsal," and "Ginny called about time for rehearsing the scene, maybe you call her back, huh?" Our Carolyn is nothing if not busy, but she could hardly have killed Gurney, and it looked to me as though she were setting herself up to be suspected. I wanted to question her about this, but once the police had finally grown tired of our presence and had begun to make those subtle hints that the party was over, and once we had straggled back into the Hall and split up, Holly and Tricia were adamant that she be left in bed.

"Oh come on," I said. "She can't be all that sick."

Holly fixed the steely eye of the Stage Manager upon me. "You know, Keith, sometimes you can be damned insensitive."

"Insensitive!" I felt that this was a bit much. "Didn't you notice how she was acting? Do you want the police carting her off for questioning?"

"If they do, it'll only be for underage drinking," said Holly. "They've got bigger things than that on their minds."

"If they haven't taken her away by now, they're not going to," said Tricia. "Let the poor girl sleep."

"'The poor girl'! What in hell has she got to worry about besides a dead hamster and too many rehearsals? That is—" I paused for suitable dramatic effect—"apart from a dead body down the hall."

"She has a hangover," said Holly. "Let her sleep."

"A hangover, my great-aunt's knee! Carolyn has never had a hangover in her life."

"There's always a first time."

"Look, I just want to know why Carolyn hates Richard Gurney."

"**Everyone** hated Richard Gurney!" hissed Pauline. "**Dickhead!**" She laughed more shrilly than was necessary, but at least I was certain that her epithet was aimed at the deceased rather than at me.

"You mean they **disliked** him," I said. "He was much too boring to hate."

"**I** hated him," said Pauline.

"You and Carolyn," I agreed. "But why?"

Pauline only laughed again, and I perceived that I had phrased my question poorly.

"Why did Carolyn hate him?"

"Because."

"Give it up, Keith," said Tricia, while Holly said "Keith, it's none of your business," and Tricia went on to say "Gosh, you're nosy tonight."

"All right, so I'm nosy." It was a concession I did not like to make, but it seemed necessary in order to placate them. "Maybe I just don't think Carolyn should get in trouble for something she didn't do."

"She's not in trouble," said Tricia. "You're the only one who thinks she is. Go to bed, Keef," she added more kindly, giving me a playful shove towards my door. "You need your beauty sleep."

It was all too clear that the three ambulatory members of the Gang of Four had me in a stalemate. They trooped militantly into Holly's room and locked the door, and as neither they nor Carolyn would respond to my entreaties, I was obliged to give up. After all, I would probably get a suitably edited version of their counsels in the morning, and in any case, experience had long since taught me that listening at dorm room doors is an inefficient means of information-gathering. I retreated to brush my teeth and contemplate the adventures of Tintin, but the adventure of The Corpse in the Trash Room continued to prey on my mind.

3

The next morning found us all rising rather sluggishly, except of course for Evan, who likes to maintain what he thinks is a more Spartan existence than the rest of us. Why he should do this on weekends, when brunch is not served until 10:30, is beyond me; but as usual I could hear him up and practicing the martial arts at what my Tintin clock informed me was the ungodly hour of seven o'clock. Most of us do not rise at seven even during the week unless we are so ill-fated as to have 8:30 language classes; in fact, Carolyn's French teachers had often jested that she had to be propped up in her chair with a stick while holding her eyes open with both hands, but now that she has passed from Modern into Medieval French, her class is held at a more civilized hour. In any case, we were all bleary-eyed as we wandered down to brunch.

But lo! we had forgotten the advent of the Spring Fair and the descent of alleged droves of high school students onto our sacred premises. As we stepped yawning into the altogether too bright morning sun, we were aghast to find clumps of middle-aged persons towing their offspring about the Quad. It is perhaps strange that we should be disturbed by this predictable sight, since we had no real objection to there being a full class of freshmen in the fall, but I believe that our feelings can be attributed to severe sensory overload. Only the night before, we had drunk heavily, heard the birth of a new limerick, and discovered a corpse where no corpse had gone before. Now, in the morning, we had wakened from an uneasy sleep punctuated by the muffled sounds of Evan's jabs and kicks, only to be blinded by the simultaneous introduction of bright light and an influx of strangers. We were entirely hesitant to go down, for fear of being beset by earnest mothers and fathers querying as to the sanitary facilities, quality of food, and **in loco parentis** policy or lack of same; and we were reluctant to look at the accompanying offspring, who would either stand diffidently to one side pretending to interest themselves in dormitory architecture, or who would aggressively collar us and ask about such things as the Politics major, whether the classes in Marxism and/or Buddhism were any good, and whether they would really have to live on campus for the entire first year.

The thought occurred to us that perhaps these had even heard, via the morning news or their car radios, of our unsavory discovery. In that case, they would be likely to rush up and interrogate us as to late-breaking developments—not, of course, imagining for a moment that it might be we our-selves who had found the corpse.

Fortunately, none of this happened. The strolling groups treated us as part of the scenery, as if we were akin to the junipers and other shrub-bery that adorned the Quad; and thus we passed safely into the dining area where we fell upon our eggs, pancakes, cereal, and bacon with groggy abandon.

Indeed, the dining room was as usual: the eggs were as runny, the pancakes as tough, the bacon as flabby as ever; the trays were as wet, the milk dis-penser as drippy, the tables as salt-sprinkled; and there was everywhere the typical subdued roar of Saturday morning brunch, a restful sound unlike the clattering and loud voices to be heard at week-day lunches and dinners. But soon there would be an announcement; at any moment the Provost or one of the preceptors would mount the stage and inform us in sober tones that Richard Gurney had been found dead, and that if any of us had any information to contribute regarding his unfortunate demise, we must immediately speak up.

And yet this, too, failed to happen. We had been among the first to fill our plates, and we lingered sleepily over our coffee, but there was no announcement. Nothing broke the routine of a lazy Saturday morning brunch. Tricia examined her mail and bemoaned the fact that her friends from high school were all marrying lobster fishermen; Pauline pointed out that this was a step up from her own high school friends, who had largely become or moved in with drug pushers and burglars; and Holly and Carolyn, who knew nothing at all about either lobster fishermen or drug pushers and burglars, freely offered their opinions on these topics. None of them paid the slightest attention to my attempts to introduce the subject of Richard Gurney.

Evan, as I expected, knew nothing of Carolyn's more personal history—he is the last person among us in whom I should expect her to confide—but he concurred that she had been asking for trouble.

"Mind you," he said, pensively rubbing his perfectly shaven chin, "she nearly always is. I'm really not sure why she's at a university anyway, since she could easily work in theater without getting a degree."

I stifled a yawn and pointed out that Carolyn is an intelligent person of scholarly interests.

"**Interests,** yes," said he, shaking a pile of salt onto the table and pushing it into the form of a smiley-face; "**interests** aren't enough. She thinks she's interested in everything, which is the same as being interested in nothing. She doesn't need to attend a university to pursue **interests**."

"Perhaps not," I said, wondering as always how he explained his own erratic and compulsive studies, "but she's here, and you are wandering from the point. I think she's hiding something about Richard Gurney."

"Why shouldn't she? Who cares what she knows about Richard Gurney so long as she didn't kill him? I'm sure Carolyn has plenty of secrets she'd rather not discuss, especially about men. They seem," he said acidly, "to be one of her major interests."

"Hardly," I protested. "I don't think she's slept with anyone all year." When Evan is in his Hall Prude role, one's natural instinct is to defend the reputations and practices of others—especially since it seemed to me that Carolyn was much too preoccupied with study and rehearsals to have time for actual dalliance.

"I would not say anything against a suitable and appropriate relationship, were she actually to form one," continued Evan, "but—"

We perceived the baleful glares of Carolyn, Holly, Tricia, and Pauline upon us.

"We're going upstairs," said Tricia, more pointedly than is her wont, and they silently arose and departed without looking at us further.

"Perhaps I have committed a **faux pas,**" remarked Evan, "but I was under the impression that they themselves were already discussing their interest in men."

"Evan," I said, "quite apart from the fact that they were discussing not their own interest in men but that of people who live any number of miles away, it is **natural** for young women to be interested in men. It is **not** natural for them to enjoy listening to you spout off about their conduct and moral betterment; they'll conclude that you dislike them."

"Dislike them! Why should I dislike them? True, they continually display their lack of moderation and restraint, but that doesn't mean that I dislike them." He looked thoroughly surprised that I should suggest such a thing, which goes to show how unaware some people are of the impression they make upon others. "On the contrary," he went on, perpetrating another smiley-face, this time with pepper, "I am quite fond of Carolyn."

I did not comment on this interesting switch from the general to the specific.

"Carolyn has a great many faults of which I am painfully aware," he continued, "but surely you cannot imagine that she's in any way connected to Richard Gurney's death. Aside from the fact that she was with the Hall practically all night, you know as well as I do that she almost **couldn't** have killed him. I'd guess that he was killed by someone who knew their martial arts, and Carolyn doesn't know anything of the sort. Her idea of self-defense would probably be to bite her attacker on the leg."

"A martial arts student, eh?" I rather liked the idea, if only because I could boast some familiarity with the topic myself. "Pity there are so many of them around. It could've been practically anyone; it could've been you or me. A little jab to the throat and Goodnight Richard Gurney."

"Precisely. But I think we can rule out most people. It wouldn't have been hard to kill him, but most people wouldn't have known where to hit him, and besides, you aren't going to tell me he was killed on location in the trash closet. Not very many people would have had the strength to move him."

"True," I agreed. "But he must have been killed nearby."

Evan rubbed his chin again, suggesting that it is never wise to shave too early in the day. "The next Hall over?" he inquired.

"Very likely," I said.

The dining room crew was beginning to pick up and wash around us, and in fact was rather ostentatiously throwing chairs atop the table to our left. We picked up our trays and left Evan's salt and pepper smiley-faces to be washed away, and returned to the dorm to contemplate the residents of the adjoining Hall, only to realize that we had no idea who lived there.

4

The Gang of Four had gone downtown; Malcolm had retreated to the library; and those Hall members who had missed out on the wake had not yet shown their faces. Our knowledge of the denizens of the next Hall appeared limited to the certainty that we did not like the music played by a certain Steve Madison; or, more specifically, that we doubted he could tell the difference between Beethoven and the Bee Gees and that we knew he was accustomed to play both at high decibels. It is true that Tricia and Carolyn are both noted for their eclectic musical tastes, and we do not dream of suggesting that they might be ignorant of the difference between the Sex Pistols and an Early Music ensemble directed by David Munro. But our only contact with the aforesaid Steve Madison had been in regard to the volume of his music, and I was not greatly desirous of speaking to him since we had personally and all too recently confronted him about his stereo.

Still—his bedroom had the distinction of being located almost next door to the trash chute; perhaps he had noticed something in between his assaults on his neighbors' ears. Evan was quite willing to speak to him, but, recollecting the dire and fiendish threats employed at the earlier meeting, I felt that we should send a neutral party on this mission. Malcolm was clearly the man we wanted, and where was he when we needed him but sequestered in the library?

Temporarily at a standstill, we applied ourselves to practicing kicks in the corridor and complaining about the intrusion of high school students onto the Quad, until to our surprise we heard the trampling of eight familiar feet returning from downtown.

"I can't believe it," Tricia was saying as she rounded the corner, "I just can't believe it. You'd think this'd be the biggest news to hit this place in years."

"It's a coverup," said Pauline.

"What's a coverup?" I inquired.

The Gang of Four arranged themselves around me, almost like players around a maypole, since they are all shorter than I am.

"There is not a single **word** about Richard Gurney in any of the papers," said Holly. "We looked all over town and there was **nothing**."

"You'd think it'd be front page news," said Carolyn, "but no, it's not as important as the new sewage treatment plant."

"Or the Sammy Hagar concert," said Tricia, who regards Sammy Hagar as a form of life roughly on a par with the slime mold.

"Or whether Lina Troyer should get tenure," said Holly.

"Who's Lina Troyer?" asked Carolyn absently, peering into a sack of used clothing that she had brought back with her.

"That lesbian Marxist woman," said Holly.

It appeared that the Gang of Four had occupied its time in scouring used clothing stores, Woolworth's, and the local bookstore-cum-café, all without encountering the slightest mention of Richard Gurney.

I refrained from pointing out that Woolworth's and used clothing outlets—no matter how fascinating in themselves—are scarcely hotbeds of criminological news. Instead, I remarked "This is Sunday, isn't it?"

"Of course it is, Keith," said Tricia.

"And Gurney died on Saturday, didn't he?"

"Yes, Keith."

"Well, then it stands to reason that he's not in the papers, doesn't it?"

There was a pause, and then Holly exclaimed, in some exasperation, "Oh, **really,** Keith! You needn't make us look like a pack of idiots!"

"Oh, **God,** Keith," said Tricia with equal irritation, having also caught my drift, "you'd think a town this size would have a decent newspaper. Sometimes I feel like we live in the middle of nowhere."

"Everybody **knows** there isn't a decent paper in this town," Holly went on. "Everybody **knows** these local papers are just a cheap substitute for kitty-litter and birdcage gravel. But not to print on **Sunday** ..."

It is well known that Holly buys the **New York Times** and, from time to time, the **Los Angeles Times;** it is perhaps not surprising that she might be unaware of local printing practices. It was less clear why Tricia, Carolyn, and Pauline, who regularly scan the entertainment news, should be ignorant of these.

"We have to wait until **Monday** to read about our own corpse?" said Tricia.

"It's altogether disgusting," said Carolyn morosely. "If a thing like this is going to happen, we should at least be able to read about it. Fuck Richard Gurney anyway." She disappeared into her room muttering something about his having been a pimple on the face of the earth, and Evan, who had silently continued to practice his kicks, raised his eyebrows.

"Quite apart from newspaper articles, which are unlikely to be correct anyway," I said, "Evan and I were wondering whether Gurney might have died in the next Hall rather than in the trash closet, and whether Steve Madison might have noticed anything untoward during the evening." We quickly outlined our thoughts regarding the situation.

"But Steve wasn't there," objected Tricia. "Remember, the police went and knocked on his door?"

"All that means is that he wasn't there at the same time we were," said Holly.

"He could've offed Gurney and split," came the muffled voice of Carolyn from behind her closed door.

"He might have heard dragging noises, at least," said Holly.

"Not if his stereo was on," said Tricia. She favored me with a deceptively limpid gaze. "Well, Keith, how come you haven't been over there interrogating him yet?"

I reminded her of the delicate situation that Evan and I had caused in our recent quest for quiet. "We had thought Malcolm might be an appropriate person, but since he's at the library and all of you are here..."

"Oh, no," said Tricia. "I'm not going to talk to that fathead. If he lived anywhere else, he'd be a frat boy."

I thought it needless to mention that, had she herself gone elsewhere and failed to come under the influence of punk rock and British folk music, she might have ended up a sorority girl.

"He's **boring**," said Pauline.

"Well, somebody ought to talk to him," said Holly. "I suppose I could do it. We had better plan out what I should ask him. Has anybody got a pencil?"

At this propitious moment, Malcolm, laden with library books of a most formidable-looking sort, entered the Hall. He was sweating freely after his trudge in the sun, but this did not deter us from falling upon him with delighted cries of "Just the person we've been wanting to see!"

"Wait a minute, what's going on? Let me put down my books, at least." Malcolm divested himself of these, wiped his face on his sleeve, and listened attentively to our proposal.

"You are probably the most tactful person here," I concluded, "and thus most likely to get useful results."

"Hardly," he demurred; "I really don't know Steve Madison at all." He wiped his brow again, as if to further dissociate himself from our neighbor by the stairs. "I'd rather not antagonize him, and since it was a Saturday night, chances are ten to one he was gone partying the whole time."

"Oh, come on Malcolm, it's very simple," said Holly. "Besides, even if he's the murderer, he's not likely to do anything to you."

"Does he even know that Gurney's dead?"

"Oh, he must; we saw Renee Gibeau downtown—she's on his Hall and **she** knew. Besides, I can go with you, and he can't really do anything worse than slam the door and turn up his stereo."

"Well," said Malcolm, with a little smile, "it looks as if I've been conscripted. All right—where are the tracts? I feel like I'm about to be a Jehovah's Witness."

"We need to ask," said Holly, taking a pencil from Tricia and writing in her firm and determined script, "when he left his room last night; who he talked to before he left; and whether he noticed any unusual sounds or traffic outside his room."

"I'll be very surprised if he noticed anything," said Malcolm, "since there's always noise by the stairs."

"Yes," said Holly, "but you never know. It can't hurt to ask."

"Especially in a friendly, subtle sort of way," I added.

"All right," said Malcolm, with a look indicating that, though he might humor us for now, he would rather be burying himself in his library books. "Let's go, but don't be surprised if he resists our blandishments and claims total ignorance."

Tricia and Pauline were now briefly tempted to follow and listen from the stairwell, but it was not difficult to dissuade them from this course of action. Evan left off kicking the wall to join us, and we began to discuss the possibility that the police might permit us a copy of their report, but were soon interrupted by the return of Malcolm and Holly.

"Nothing," said Holly. "Dead nothing."

"I'm afraid," said Malcolm, "that Steve Madison does not recall anything remotely out of the ordinary."

"He was home, though?"

"For part of the evening," said Holly. "He claimed not to be able to remember which part."

"Suspicious," said Pauline, with satisfaction.

"Lamebrained," said Tricia.

"It wasn't that he had no idea," countered Malcolm, "it was that he had not bothered to note the time. He was quite pleasant about it, actually. He said he thought he had studied for an hour or two, or more, and thought he had gone to the coffee shop at least once, and probably to the cigarette machine, and perhaps to the bathroom, and eventually over to a friend's to smoke joints, and from there to another friend's, and there you have it."

"He said he thought various people had knocked on his door during the evening," continued Holly, "but he wasn't sure which of them did last night and which did the night before or the night before that, since people knock on his door a lot."

"I'll bet they do," said Tricia.

"Oh, there's no need to be so hard on him," said Malcolm. "He seems like a decent sort apart from his love of noise. I think he honestly can't remember which night so-and-so came by to borrow his typewriter, and when the other so-and-so offered him the especially potent 'shrooms, and when he was asked to contribute to a kegger or to save the whales."

"They all seemed like the kind of depressingly ordinary interruptions that happen to all of us," agreed Holly.

"He invited us in for beer," said Malcolm, "but we thought we had drunk enough last night not to want any more until at least seven o'clock."

"Ingratiating," I said.

"He's a nice boy," said Holly, "just dull. He has a Monet waterlily print on his wall."

I gathered that the Monet print was considered a point in his favor rather than otherwise.

"Well, either he was in his room or he wasn't," remarked Evan, "and either he noticed something that he mistakenly considers unimportant, or he noticed nothing. Either way, I cannot see that we're any further ahead than we were before."

"We know that he has a Monet print," said Pauline sarcastically; being a tolerant sort, I did not employ my martial arts training on her.

5

"We must look at this logically," I said. "From a logical perspective, we do not care whether Steve Madison has a Monet print." Choruses of "DUHHH!" greeted me, but I ignored them. "From a logical perspective, we do not care what any of the furnishings of his room look like. We do not care whether he likes Giotto or Kandinsky."

"He likes Lainey Silver," said Holly.

"Not personally, I hope!" giggled Tricia.

"We don't care whether he likes Lainey Silver either," said Evan.

"Lainey was a good artist before she took so much acid," remarked Pauline.

"We do not care whether Lainey was a good artist," I said. "We are interested in clues." Carolyn, who had emerged from her room again, yawned, but I went on. "Was there anything unusual about Steve Madison's bedroom? About his behavior?"

Now Holly yawned. "I didn't expect him to have a Monet print, but you don't seem to want to hear about that. He didn't have his stereo on, but he doesn't usually in the afternoon anyway. What more do you want?"

"Male Caucasian, dark hair, boring exterior," suggested Carolyn. "Normal height and weight, no visible zits, major unknown. Turns out to keep iguanas in his bedroom," she added in a typical burst of invention.

"Returning to the logical perspective," I said, aware that Steve Madison does not in fact keep iguanas in his bedroom, "let us query as to time, opportunity, and motive. We might start from the general and move to the particular."

"How general?" said Tricia.

"Well, we don't know yet just when Gurney was killed, so that makes it difficult to ask about opportunity, but obviously the murderer had to have a motive."

The Gang of Four looked at me as if I had offered to teach them how to count to ten.

"Gurney was a jerk," said Carolyn. "Anyone could have a motive."

I coughed delicately. "Normal persons do not go about killing people for being jerks."

"Tempting though it may be," added Evan.

"Yes, well, some of us have been tempted any number of times," said Carolyn pointedly.

"He was a jerk, but I don't think many people spent enough time with him to get that mad at him," commented Holly.

"Yeah, everyone knew he was kind of a turkey, but it wasn't like he went around getting into fights with them," agreed Tricia. "They just kind of avoided him so they didn't have to listen to his dumb remarks."

"He was boring," said Holly, "boring and vapid. Nobody kills people for being boring and vapid."

"He thought he was a stud," said Tricia. "Remember how he used to wear those tight jeans over those fake Frye boots?"

"Someone murdered him for a reason," I said. "If he offended them, he must have offended them pretty deeply."

"A psychopath," suggested Malcolm with a grin.

"Dripping in blood and gore and twisted desires," said Carolyn. "Forget psychopaths, Gurney didn't even look dead when we found him. Besides, if it's a psychopath I'll have to start locking my door at night. Make it an act of international espionage instead. He was passing secrets to the Russians, and the CIA caught on and bopped him."

"Your levity is scarcely appropriate," said Evan.

"Why shouldn't he have been passing secrets to the Russians? It's more likely than gang warfare."

"Secrets about what?" snorted Holly. "Dormitory management?"

"Well," I said, "there are always the familiar motives of greed and passion."

"What would he have that anybody'd want?" said Tricia. "His waterbed?"

"He might've had practically anything," said Holly. "At least, anything small and portable. I never heard that his suite was anything remarkable to look at."

"Believe me, it wasn't!" said Carolyn.

"Gold and jewels," suggested Pauline hastily.

"Famous paintings and books stolen from Special Collections," said Tricia.

"Massive quantities of drugs," said Carolyn. "Automatic weapons and instruments of torture."

"Unfortunately we have no idea what he might have had," said Malcolm, "which makes it difficult to guess what might have been stolen."

"Solid gold cufflinks inherited from a remote ancestor who got them from Catherine the Great," offered Tricia.

Malcolm then inquired whether cufflinks had been invented yet in Catherine's day, but received no satisfactory answer despite the Gang of Four's shared interest in costume history.

"Perhaps we should examine passion rather than greed," suggested Evan.

I was surprised that he would want to discuss anything so potentially sordid, but Evan is a surprising youth. "What sort of passion did you have in mind?" I asked.

"Well, passion comes in a variety of forms," he said, predictably backing away from anything so crude as the ordinary sexual variety. "Anger is a familiar one."

I refrained from pointing out that most people are not as intimate with anger as he is.

"Anger by itself isn't good enough, Evan," said Holly.

"Otherwise," muttered Carolyn to Pauline, "we already would've killed Evan."

Pauline snickered appreciatively.

"Sex," continued Holly, "**there's** passion. I mean, a person can be passionate about their career or something" (Holly has been known to be that), "but sex is more likely."

"He probably wanted to fuck someone who didn't like him," said Carolyn.

I felt this was an improbable notion if I had ever heard one. "Rapists are more likely to kill their victims than vice versa," I said.

"Not rape, he just aroused a passion of disgust in his intended," she retorted.

"Rather far-fetched, don't you think?" asked Malcolm.

"Sure, but anything's possible. He was a sleaze."

"You seem to know a lot about him," remarked Evan.

"**Everyone** knows that Gurney was sleazy," said Holly with great hauteur.

"Not **that** sleazy," I said. "How many people do you know that he's slept with? Or even come on to?"

The Gang of Four was silent.

"We all know he was sleazy," I continued, "but he did not seem to be very successful about it. The man was not popular; he couldn't even get people to go to his asinine sherry parties."

"Liz MacKellar went to one once," said Tricia. "He told her what gorgeous hair she has."

"Liz's misguided escapades can hardly concern us," protested Evan. "We are speaking of motives for murder, not whether Liz was foolish enough to go to one of Richard Gurney's sherry parties."

"Which Hall does Liz live on, anyway?" I asked. "It would be rather convenient if she lived on the same one as Steve Madison."

"She does," said Tricia.

"Aha," I said. "So that means Gurney was their preceptor. Another Hall to suspect."

"Only if they pay attention to their preceptor," said Malcolm. "Who's ours?"

"**Gurney** was ours!" said Holly.

Perhaps at this juncture it would be as well for me to explain the administrative setup of our college. Our dorms, as already mentioned, are divided into Halls, which—with the exception of our wing—are overseen by Resident Assistants, popularly known as RAs. Our wing being small, all four floors are under the direction of one RA, a psych major named JoAnne. The Halls are then grouped in random threes and put under the jurisdiction of a preceptor, who for his or her trouble is allotted an entire suite on ground floor.

The preceptors are typically grad students or junior faculty members, or occasionally former students who cannot bear to drag themselves away to find a "real" job. Gurney was a grad student, who claimed to be studying the works of Kurt Vonnegut; neither he nor anyone else appeared to take this very seriously. Had he been a serious scholar ... Well, I do not wish to cast aspersions on Vonnegut, whose works I enjoy, but there was no question that Gurney was not a serious scholar.

In any case, above the preceptors there is the Housing Coordinator, whose job it is to assign students to rooms, choose the RAs and preceptors, and to generally keep the dorms in good order. Then, of course, there is the Provost, who has charge of the college as a whole, and the Chancellor, who heads the entire university. I did not think the Chancellor was likely to be involved in the murder, or even to know who Gurney was, but it did occur to me that perhaps the activities of the Provost and the other preceptors should be looked into.

"I wonder how the other preceptors feel about Gurney?" I said.

"They thought he was a bozo, Keith, just like we did," said Tricia.

"Very likely," I said, "but do you know that for a fact?"

"Well, no, but **they** had to have meetings with him about whatever preceptors have meetings about, so they had to listen to whatever dumb remarks he made whether they liked it or not. Gosh, imagine having to be one of his RAs and being expected to plan social events with him!"

"At least **we** plan our own events," said Holly.

"Yeah, we don't need any help with that," said Carolyn.

Desultory conversation with few redeeming features followed, and before long it was dinnertime. I was somewhat irritated to realize that I had managed to fritter away so much valuable study time without having become any better informed about Richard Gurney's death, but I reminded myself that the pursuit of knowledge is arduous, and that one cannot expect to solve crimes without enduring some frustration. Malcolm had eventually made good his desire to study, but he is a more reclusive person than some, and his interest in Gurney was clearly limited. When five o'clock stole upon us, we sighed, gathered up our meal cards, and returned to the dining room.

The roving high school students had by now largely gone home, and the Quad was returning to normal. Balloons and paper cups here and there indicated a slight disruption of routine, but on the whole all was as usual. We devoured our falafel and constructed sundaes of tottering height and gooey magnificence, then dispersed, some to study, Pauline to her room to continue work on a monumental canvas of Aunt Jemima dancing with the Jolly Green Giant, and Holly and Carolyn to rehearsal.

As Holly and Carolyn rushed in and out of each other's rooms in search of notebooks, sweaters, and gloves, I reflected upon what a fortunate thing it was that I had chosen not to be a Theater major. For although the historian must spend considerable time researching, libraries and archives are usually accessible during normal daytime hours, and their seating, though not always comfortable, is generally adequate; whereas persons involved in theater must expect to be at rehearsals at any time of day or night without respect to mealtimes, bus schedules, or holidays, and must endure unheated rooms, leaky roofs, dangerous wiring, and incompetent or temperamental companions. I would not soon forget my experience of a performance in which a "barndoor" fell suddenly from its Fresnel and nearly brained the leading man; I had been waiting offstage for my own admittedly minor entrance, and though I was less visible than the leading man, I was standing under just as many Fresnels, all of which had been put up by the same scatterbrained assistant.

"See you, Keith," yelled Holly and Carolyn. Muttering their usual complaints about their director, they ran out the door and down the stairs; I returned to my room and my studies.

6

I was not destined to study long that night. When I ventured out of my room around eight o'clock to pour hot water on my tea bag, I encountered Evan diligently brushing his teeth. I did not ask why he was brushing his teeth when we had finished dinner two hours before and it was not yet bedtime; I had long ago discovered that Evan showered and brushed his teeth with unusual frequency.

"Hello, Keith," he said cheerily. His words were somewhat indistinct, as befitted a man with a toothbrush in his mouth; I stationed myself at the farthest sink in case any foam should fly in the direction of my tea.

"This business with Gurney is pretty nasty," he continued. "I don't like the fact that the college hasn't even announced the murder yet. Do they imagine no one knows?"

"Considering that we found the body," I said, "they would be out of their minds to think that."

"Ferdinand **is** out of his mind," said Evan. Ferdinand is our provost.

"Well, he's not overly bright, except in academic matters," I agreed. "And even there I have my doubts."

Evan rinsed his mouth with great thoroughness and patted his towel meticulously to his lips. "I wonder if Ferdinand did it."

"Why would Ferdinand do it?"

"Why does Ferdinand do anything?"

He had a point. "Ferdinand does things for his own silly reasons," I said. "Sometimes they work for the greater good of mankind and sometimes they don't. There's no question that his dinner parties were more amusing than Richard Gurney's sherry parties."

"Yes," said Evan, "there's no question at all of that. I just wonder whether he might have done the murder himself, which would explain why we haven't been treated to an official briefing."

"Yes," I said, "but **why** would he do it?" I thought the idea rather charming, but unlikely. It seemed to me that Ferdinand spent too much of his time poring over his slide collection and trying to look urbane. I could imagine him carrying on intrigues with other people's wives, but not committing a murder.

"Gurney might have discovered something damaging about him," said Evan. "I'm sure Ferdinand has secrets, some of which would be embarrassing to a man in his position."

"I don't think most of Ferdinand's secrets are all that secret," I said. "When you've been here a few more years you'll probably know *and* be bored by them."

Evan scowled at the idea that he might stay in school as long as I had. He tends to think the curriculum insufficiently rigorous, and blames his frequent changes of major on the inadequacies of the departments involved.

"Well," I said, "besides Ferdinand, there are Theo, the other preceptors, and Gurney's three RAs."

"Can you imagine Theo killing anyone?" said Evan.

Theo Roth, the Housing Coordinator, is an obliging sort in his late twenties. It was true that he seemed to like most people, and that they seemed to like him. He always seemed to do his best to give people the rooms they wanted, and in the evening he was always good for casual conversation.

"There are the other preceptors and the RAs," I said.

At this point we suddenly heard voices from the hallway.

"It was really gross," Tricia was saying. "I mean, it wasn't like there was blood all over or anything like that, but it was still gross. Holly opened the door, and he was just sitting there like a dummy or something on top of the trash can!"

"Gee," said a voice I recognized as that of Liz MacKellar, "it must have been horrible."

"Believe me, it was!" said Tricia. "Oh, gosh-darn it, where the hell did I put my key?"

Evan and I stepped unobtrusively into the corridor.

"Oh, hi, Keith, hi Evan," said Tricia. She did not sound altogether pleased to see us. "I'm just going to lend Liz my Petula Clark record."

"Petula Clark?" said Evan disbelievingly.

"Petula Clark?" I echoed. Surely Petula Clark was a little before their time, or at least rose to stardom in their kindergarten days.[1]

"Tricia was telling me all about how you discovered the body," exclaimed Liz. "It must've been really awful. God, I never would've thought something like that would ever happen in **our** dorm!"

Tricia located her key and unlocked the door. "All right, Petula, where are you?" she muttered. "Let me see, you wanted **Mary Poppins** too."

"I'd love to hear **Mary Poppins,**" said Liz. "Did he look really dead?"

This non-sequitur staggered me, but only for a second. "Not very," I said.

"God, it's so hard to believe!" Liz exclaimed, taking the Petula Clark and **Mary Poppins** records from Tricia. "I remember when he gave a sherry party so that everybody on his Halls could get acquainted, only hardly anybody showed up. It wasn't nearly as fun as Gordon's horoscope party last year. He just kept pouring more and more sherry whether we wanted it or not and kept trying to make us eat more cheese and crackers even though it was right before dinner, and he kept putting his arm around Zoe Vogel and she kept wiggling away."

"Zoe's gay," I said disgustedly. "I thought everyone knew that."

"Well, I knew it," said Liz, "but obviously **he** didn't. He was just all over her, telling her what great hair she had and asking her what she liked to do, if she liked to go camping or what."

"Poor Zoe," I said.

"I know," said Liz. "She finally left, and then Rhoda started making nasty remarks about her."

"Who's Rhoda?" said Evan.

Tricia made a face. "Oh, she's this annoying person who was on the Girls' Hall with me freshman year. She's always whining about something."

"I don't think Richard Gurney's sherry agreed with Rhoda," said Liz. "Although I think she must've drank an awful lot of it. She went on and on about how she and Zoe had been in Lina Troyer's class together and how the only reason Zoe did well in the class was because she was sleeping with Lina. Rhoda seemed to think Lina didn't like **her** because she wasn't gay or something."

"It wouldn't take that for someone not to like Rhoda," said Tricia.

"It was embarrassing," said Liz. "It looked to me like Rhoda just wanted to get back at Zoe for Zoe having done so well in Lina's class. She kept on and on about how hard she'd worked and how none of it was any use because Lina hated straight women."

"Oh, bullshit," said Tricia. "I don't know about Lina Troyer, but I know about Rhoda. She's too busy complaining to study."

Not being personally acquainted with the odious Rhoda, I began to lose interest in the conversation. Zoe I knew and liked; Lina Troyer was politically interesting as a lesbian Marxist up for tenure; but I had to force myself to remember that Rhoda might also be of interest.

"Do you think Rhoda might have killed Gurney?" I inquired.

Tricia and Liz started to laugh.

"He'd be more likely to have killed her!" said Liz.

"She wasn't taking classes from Gurney!" said Tricia simultaneously.

"Well, we have to consider these things," I said. "He didn't kill **himself.**"

"No, more's the pity," said Tricia. "Just think, we wouldn't have **anything** to worry about if that were the case!" Then she seemed to recollect the gravity of the situation. She looked perturbed and quite unhappy, for Tricia is a kindly person at heart. "You know," she said, "it's really hard to believe he's dead."

---

1. Unbeknownst to me, Petula Clark has remained very popular, and continued to perform for decades after Tricia lent Liz her record.

7

There was a small silence. It was true that it was surprisingly difficult to remember that Richard Gurney was really dead; it was difficult to remember that he would stay that way for all time, and that his death was a terrible thing. Somehow Gurney was not able, even in death, to be a very serious person. Even in death he remained a fool, the kind of person whose murderer hadn't even left him lying decently on the floor or on the bed, hadn't taken the trouble to sneak him onto a truck and dump him in a ravine or cover him with leaves, but had put him in the trash closet sitting on a garbage can as if he were a sack of old newspapers or a freshman in a stupor.

I reflected that if Richard Gurney had been run over by a car, or stabbed in an alley by a mugger, we might have had an easier time believing that he was dead, but we would still not be able to refrain from making rude remarks about him. We would still remember him as the sort of person who insisted on pouring people too much sherry, who persisted in making advances to gay women.

If Theo Roth or even Ferdinand had been murdered, we would have been aghast. And if Tricia or Liz or Malcolm or Holly or Carolyn or any number of other people had been murdered, we would have been unable to function, crawling about the Hall in mourning and wandering desolately into one another's rooms in search of comfort. But even though we had seen Richard Gurney dead, we had trouble believing that it was real.

"I wonder whether he'll be the only one," said Liz soberly.

Feeling chilled, all three of us walked her back to her room, just in case the murderer might take a fancy to her as well. She didn't have much in common with Gurney, but it suddenly seemed better to be safe than sorry, because who knew why Gurney might have been killed? Liz promised to return Petula and **Mary Poppins** shortly, and we listened for the click of her door locking before we turned to leave. Then, quietly, we returned to our own rooms and locked ourselves in to sleep.

This somber mood, of course, did not last long. In the morning the world reverted to its normal aspect. The sun was out, we had classes to attend, and Richard Gurney's death again seemed like a fantastical interruption, the sort of bizarre and ridiculous thing that might impinge upon our weekend gatherings. Beast's funeral and Richard Gurney's death seemed like two events of one kind, things that had nothing to do with the everyday world of seminars, papers, lost library books, and missed lunches. Besides, no mention of Gurney had been made in the college; there were still no announcements, no Xeroxed flyers warning us to be on the alert. Nor, insofar as we knew, had any television crews been by to film the yellow plastic police tape across the trash closet door. Could such an event be real without drawing the attention of the media? I applied myself in class and in the library as best I could in order to make up for a weekend that had totally lacked academic focus, but of course my concentration was not what it might have been.

"Keith!" said Holly as I returned to the Hall in late afternoon, "It's in the papers!"

"Which papers?" I asked, unlocking my door and throwing my books onto the bed.

"The local papers. The **Banner,** specifically. Look, isn't this a stupid article?"

I took the paper from her and looked at the small column—paragraph, to be specific—to which she pointed. It was not, indeed, very informative. It said:

MAN FOUND DEAD

Richard Gurney, a Preceptor at the University, was found dead late Saturday night near his on-campus residence. Police spokesmen declined to state the cause of death, but said that foul play was suspected. Gurney was 31.

"**We** could have written a more detailed article than that!" said Holly, and I agreed.

"The most interesting thing about this article **is** its lack of detail," I said.

Holly grimaced. "That's just because the **Banner** is an utterly worthless paper."

"The police probably didn't tell them very much."

"Oh well." She sighed dramatically. "I'm not impressed with either the police or the newspapers in this town. Have you seen Tricia lately?"

"Not since last night—why?"

"Oh, I just wanted to ask her something ..."

Somehow I had the feeling that Holly was being a trifle evasive, despite the fact that she had asked similar questions and been similarly vague countless times before. I wondered whether my curiosity about Gurney's death had begun to make me wonder about things that I would normally ignore—the Gang of Four is always up to something, and not necessarily anything of any interest to anyone else. I had known them to indulge in lengthy consultations about trips downtown to buy gummi bears, to scheme about whose faces to draw into their costume history illustrations, and to write elaborate notes about the bagels they planned to eat at the coffee shop.

"How was rehearsal last night?" I inquired.

Holly looked even more disgusted than she had about the newspaper. "Oh, those actors are no help at all. We were there until one, and then we just missed a bus, and then we didn't get to bed until about three, so we were **rather** late to Greg's class this morning. I'm going to have to start laying down the law to those people about time."

Once again, I was glad not to have majored in theater. Instead, and this I was also glad of, I had my martial-arts class to look forward to after dinner. It would be fun, it would be active, and it would not go past 9:30.

Evan and I enjoyed our class tremendously. He took it much more seriously than I did, practicing incessantly and paying close attention to Chong's lectures on diet, but we both found it stimulating. As Chong has his own particular method, going well beyond just martial arts, we were also inclined to argue over which of his teachings were inspired and which were simply lunatic.

Upon entering the practice room—a medium sized, wooden-floored room next to the main gym—we began to warm up. The other students were tossing their backpacks and purses along the wall and stretching, and two or three of them were sitting on a table talking to Chong. Through the walls, I could hear the familiar sounds of basketball and the jazz dance class piano, as well as thumps and stomps and now and then the dance teacher stridently chanting "ONE two three" and other, more arcane, phrases.

"I don't suppose anyone here knew Gurney," I said to Evan.

"Probably not," he agreed. "Not unless they live in our dorm or something."

I looked around the room. Did anyone in it live in our dorm? Ours is not one of the skyscraper variety, and I thought I probably knew most of its inhabitants by sight, but I had never bothered to categorize my classmates by dorm or college. I noted Zoe Vogel, certainly a conscientious student; Norman Rice, a very poor and uncoordinated one who only showed up because his girlfriend was in the class; and Nancy Ishimatsu and Dan Ward. I did not think any of them were very likely to have killed Richard Gurney, and, of course, why should the killer be in the same martial-arts class as we were? There were other sections of martial arts offered on campus, and further classes downtown, and besides, the murderer need not have taken a class in years. He might have taken a class at the age of fifteen or sixteen, or have taken one at some other school and transferred here. The murderer might of course have been a woman, but if so, I thought surely a big woman, for though the deed itself did not require size, the planting of the body argued it. And there were not even any big women in the class—certainly not Zoe or Nancy or Norman Rice's girlfriend.

Class began, and I abandoned my speculations, not wanting them to distract me from my kicks and jabs and defensive maneuvers. I noticed that Zoe was sitting on the sidelines and that the jazz piano was more intrusive than usual, but then I forced myself to concentrate.

At the break, gulping tepid water and wondering why half the class smoked, I heard Zoe apologizing to Chong.

"I'm sorry," she was saying, "I thought I'd feel up to working, but I'm having trouble even sitting here watching. I just hope it's not that flu that's going around."

"It's a nasty flu," agreed Nancy. "You ought to go home and go to bed and take massive vitamins."

"I guess I should," said Zoe. She did sound ill. "I don't want to miss Wednesday too, not to mention the rest of my classes."

She went out, looking as though she might be sick on her way back. Evan offered to walk with her, but she refused, so we went back to class.

The Hall was in a minor uproar when we returned. Even at a distance, we could hear Tricia saying "Well, if they'd stop sticking their big noses into everything we do! I was all set to interrogate Liz about her Hall when **they** came along and distracted her onto Gurney's stupid sherry party, as though there was anything new to hear about **that.**"

"They think they know everything," agreed Holly. "It wouldn't be so bad if it was just Keith, but when Evan joins in ..."

Hearing ourselves reviled, we paused.

"After all, it's only obvious we have to find out who Gurney actually spent time with," said Carolyn.

"Yes, and if **they** start looking into that—" said Tricia.

"Exactly!" said Holly.

We looked at each other and frowned.

"I thought I had it perfectly set up to go borrow Renee's anthro book and ask her how she heard about the murder," Tricia continued, "and even though she wasn't there it was still fine that Liz came along and wanted to borrow my records, because I could ask her questions too, but no, **they** had to show up. Boy."

It did not seem that we could really stand about listening any longer and still make a convincing entrance, so at this point we strode in affecting an air of great casualness.

8

"Hello, Keith, hello Evan," said Holly and Tricia with no enthusiasm at all. Pauline giggled rudely, and Carolyn inquired how class had been.

"Class," said Evan, "was very much as usual. There was no reason for it to be otherwise."

They did not look any happier than before at this.

"And what of your rehearsals?" he went on.

"**FOR**tunately, we didn't have to go tonight," said Holly. "It was cancelled and we had to call all the actors to tell them."

"Gave us a chance to catch up on the rest of our work for once," said Carolyn. "I have about three

French poems due and a paper on Roman drama. Seneca and his kin were disgusting people. Killed their characters right and left."

"Yes, enough of that going on in our daily life, I suppose," I said.

"Well, yes," said Carolyn. "That too. But Seneca is repulsive. If I have to read plays full of blood and guts, give me the Jacobeans, or **The Revenger's Tragedy,** or something like that."

"As far as I'm concerned," said Holly, "all those blood-and-guts plays are the same, and they're ridiculous to stage. Messing with all that fake blood and having to launder the costumes every day ... One murder per play is enough, thank you, unless it's something like **Hamlet** where half the people get poisoned and the other half are run through with rapiers so thin that the blood can't get out."

"Well, plays from most periods don't require actual gore onstage," said Carolyn, "no matter how many people they kill. It's the Roman ones and the revenge plays that wallow in guts and have one character yanking out the other's heart and all that kind of thing."

"The sort of thing you might expect from societies that entertained their citizens with gladiators and public beheadings and burnings and disembowelings," I said.

"This is beginning to turn my stomach," said Tricia.

"It's already turned mine," said Holly. "Let's go to the coffee shop and talk about something else."

"Like Richard Gurney?" said Evan.

Pauline giggled again, and the other three made faces.

"I'm sick of the whole topic," said Holly. "He's dead, and pretty soon the police will catch whoever did it, and life will go back to normal."

It was a nice speech, but of course she didn't mean it. She and the rest of the Gang of Four were clearly up to something, and for some reason they didn't want me and Evan in on it.

By late Tuesday morning, word of the murder seemed to have finally hit the greater student body. Not everyone knew, and most people were only aware of the vaguest details, but the news was out, and there was considerable murmuring and muttering. People would say "Did you hear about the murder?" and their friends would say "Yeah, but only that there was one—what happened?" And the first person would say "Well, I don't really know, but I think it happened on the other side of campus." Or someone would say "Was there a rape involved?" and the other person would say "Hell no, it was some guy, a proctor or a preceptor or something like that."

After returning from a quick trip to the library, where a simultaneously alarming and gratifying pile of interlibrary loan books awaited me (**why,** I asked myself peevishly as I wrestled them into my backpack, had I been so possessed as to think I would have time to read or even skim all of these?), I settled myself and the books on my bed, sought the appropriate notebook and my favorite pen, and attempted to immerse myself in the normally fascinating world of Voltaire and the Enlightenment. But from my window I could see groups of students going into the College Office, and other groups standing in front of the Provost's office. After a while I went down to the College Office myself, as the secretaries were old friends of mine, and I listened to them telling one group after another that yes, Richard Gurney had been murdered on Saturday night, and that no, they didn't know much more than that but the police were working on the case and the Provost would be making an announcement at dinner, and no, it didn't seem to be the work of a maniac so yes, it was probably safe to go on with your daily life if you took reasonable precautions. But no, nobody knew **why** Gurney had been killed. And so on.

The College Office seemed hotter than usual with all of these worried students drifting in and out asking the same questions over and over, some of them even asking their own questions more than once as if unsure of the answers they had received. The secretaries did not seem to be getting much work done, and they looked rather frazzled.

"At least we're not getting forty million phone calls," said one.

"Yet," said the other. "We ought to make you answer all the questions, Keith," she went on. "You always know what's going on—I'm not surprised **you** found the body."

I was glad that for the moment there were no other students in the office. "There's no need to tell everyone who found him," I said. "We like to lead a quiet life on our Hall."

"Quiet, my foot!" she said. "You have the wildest Quiet Hall I've ever heard of. Your Hall gets up to as much mischief as any party Hall. We know who put that sculpture in front of Ferdinand's door. We know who cranks up 'I Wanna Be Sedated' every time the fire alarm goes off."

At least she wasn't bringing up the time we'd barricaded Carolyn into her room and kept egging her to open her door, during which incident Holly and Tricia kept wailing that she'd get claustrophobia or have to use the bathroom, and Carolyn herself retaliated by putting on a record of Korean opera that would have woken the dead.

"We study harder than you ever did," I said.

"If that was true, you'd've graduated on time like I did," said the one who had been on my Hall freshman year.

"You just breezed on through without thinking twice," I said. "Look how much more work I'll have put into my degree."

"Yeah, and look how much more of a student loan you'll have to pay back when you're through!"

"I want to know what you were up to when you found the body," said the other. "I've never heard of an entire Hall taking out the trash in unison."

"Yup, seems pretty fishy to me."

"If you must know," I said, "we were conducting a wake for Carolyn's hamster."

They both burst out laughing at this.

"Keith, that's really priceless! Where do you get these ideas?"

"A wake! God in heaven, how absurd!"

"You needn't tell the whole world about it," I said. "It seemed like a perfectly good idea at the time. Relief Proctor Sally provided an elegiac limerick for the animal."

"Sally wasn't there when you found the body, I suppose."

"No," I admitted. "She couldn't take that long away from her rounds."

"I wonder where she was when the murder took place?"

"Just when **did** the murder take place?" I asked.

"Keith, the police don't tell us things like that; we're only poor suffering college secretaries who have to allay everyone's fears about being murdered in their beds."

"Gurney wasn't murdered in his bed."

"You know what I mean! Besides, who knows where he really **was** murdered?"

"Yeah, he could've been murdered on your Hall, Keith. 'The Hall that swills together, kills together.'"

"That was repulsive, Kathy," said Linda.

"Well, it can't be 'the Hall that prays together, slays together,' since we know they don't pray."

"I don't know where you get these perverse ideas," I said. "It must be the result of having been a Lit major."

"Listen to him! He has a wake for a hamster and then has the gall to accuse Lit majors of being perverse. Hey, speaking of local scandals, d'you suppose the powers that be will hear about Lina Troyer's little affair in time to deny her tenure?"

"They will if you don't keep your voice down when you talk about it!"

"Faculty and staff are always having affairs with students," said Linda. "They always have and always will, it's a law of nature."

"Yes, but they're not **supposed** to, especially lesbian Marxists who are up for tenure."

"I suppose you've both been having affairs with students right and left," I said.

"Hardly," said Linda, who is married.

"It's of no importance to me," I said politely. "I'd much rather know whether Sally noticed anything odd on her rounds."

"I'm sure the police have already gotten her on that one," said Kathy, and then, "Oh, hell, more students!"

"Yes, and we haven't even pried any good details out of this ox here," said Linda. "Get out, Keith, we've got work to do. If we spent all our time gossiping with you about hamsters, we'd never get anything done!"

I forbore to point out that this was only obvious, and, bowing and smiling sweetly at them, left the office.

I thought I would go and visit Theo Roth next, but unfortunately he was out. Oh well—if the murder wasn't solved by Friday night, I could ask Relief Proctor Sally a few questions when she came on duty. Questions such as when she had first noticed the sign on the trash closet ... if, of course, she had noticed it at all. Kathy was probably correct in supposing that the police had already asked Sally this sort of thing, but the police had not troubled to pass the information on to us. In fact, the police were not passing any information to speak of on to anyone, which made me wonder whether they had found so many clues that they were simply waiting for the murderer to stumble, or whether they believed it a waste of time to tell the general populace what was going on. Either way, I thought it tiresome.

At dinner, Ferdinand mounted the stage as planned, right in the middle of dessert.

"Look," said Tricia excitedly, "here it comes!"

"About time," said Carolyn.

"I don't suppose he'll have anything new to say," sniffed Holly.

Ferdinand looked as though he expected to find a microphone onstage, but of course there is only a microphone at special events. He stood for a moment while everyone thumped the tables and rattled the silverware in the traditional announcement-greeting manner—a rapid, thunderous left-right drumming on the table edges and a slower clanging of spoons against glassware—and then, when the noise subsided, he said "Good evening."

"Good evening, Ferdinand," shouted everyone, or nearly everyone; Tricia shouted this enthusiastically and then muttered "Get on with it, Ferdinand," but most of the rest of us sat impatiently leaning on our elbows, waiting.

"As many of you already know," said Ferdinand in his best oratorical style, "a tragic event recently occurred in Damson House. Richard Gurney, a preceptor there, was found dead on Saturday night."

Amid the murmuring that followed this pronouncement, Carolyn could be heard to remark "Anyone would think that Gurney being found was the tragic part!"

"I know," said Holly.

"Yeah," said Tricia, "it was all right for him to die, but we went and turned it into a tragedy. Thanks a lot, Ferdinand."

"Richard Gurney," Ferdinand went on, "was murdered."

As might have been expected, there was more than mere murmuring after **this** announcement. It was a good while before Ferdinand could continue, during which time our table made its share of snide remarks about the laboriousness of his delivery.

"Speed it up," said Evan.

"Tell us something we don't know," said Tricia.

"Bring on the audio-visuals," said Pauline.

"It's not an easy job," remarked Malcolm with a little smile.

Ferdinand took another breath and continued. "It is not yet known," he said, "who killed Richard Gurney."

This time there was near-silence, and, after an unnecessary pause for suspense, he delivered his next sentence.

"If anyone has any information relating to this unfortunate event, he or she should **immediately** report to my office, and I will speak to the appropriate authorities. Meanwhile, although we do not have any reason to believe that anyone is in danger, the reverse is also true: we do not have any reason to believe that anyone is automatically safe."

"This means everyone'll be walking around in total uncertainty," muttered Holly irritably.

"Thus," said Ferdinand, "while it is probably safe for you to go to class as usual and generally go about your business, it is vital that you be extremely cautious. Please walk with as many people as possible, and please lock your doors at all times. We must not allow this to happen again. Thank you."

He made as if to leave the stage, but people began to yell questions.

"Where'd you find him?"

"How was he killed?"

"Have the police got any suspects?"

"How come we haven't heard about this before now?"

Ferdinand hesitated, and then said "I'm very sorry, but I cannot answer all of your questions. The police are investigating the matter, and in the meantime we must all be very careful."

He stepped down from the stage, and Malcolm said "I notice that he forgot to make the customary remarks about how much we'll all miss the deceased, and what a tragedy it is that someone so young should die."

"Yes, he seems to have forgotten that part of his speech," I said. "Gives you the feeling he didn't think Gurney was much of a loss."

Just then we were surprised by a familiar, rotund figure above us.

"There you are," she exclaimed. "I've been looking for you all over."

9

"All of us?" I asked.

"Of course all of you," she said. "I assume all of you found the body."

Mariah Sebastian is a reporter for the University paper; before moving downtown, she had lived two floors below us.

"Well, don't announce it so loudly," I said. "We don't need the whole dining room rushing over here to ask the questions Ferdinand wouldn't answer."

"I can interview you though, can't I?" she said.

We looked at each other, and then back at Mariah.

"Sure, why not?" we said.

"But let's make it up in our lounge or something," I said.

This met with her approval, and so we all put our trays in order and, throwing our leftovers and napkins in the trash, deposited the washables on the kitchen conveyor belt. Tricia and Pauline, who knew some of the kitchen crew, yelled their greetings down the belt, and we went on up to the lounge. Luckily we had not taken **all** of the furniture into the phone alcove; luckily there remained two sofas and a beanbag chair of mysterious origin.

The eight of us settled on these sofas and in the beanbag chair in varying degrees of formality. Mariah put her notebook on her knee and tested her pen, and said "Okay, this is a big story, and for some reason it's just starting to come out days after it happened. I mean, Richard Gurney got killed on Saturday night and this is already fucking Tuesday-after-dinner. The paper comes out tomorrow, and if we'd heard about this in decent time we could have had most of the article typeset by now as opposed to being faced with an all-nighter of the speed and caffeine variety. But shit, we only heard about this because this morning Marcus was glancing through last night's **Banner** and happened upon the minuscule item **they** chose to print on the subject. I mean, is that any way to get news? We have a history of scooping the **Banner** out of existence, not that that's difficult because they're such a crappy paper, but why's the **Banner** getting in ahead of us on a university news item? It'd be one thing if it were just a matter of them publishing more often than we do, but when we have to get our news **from** them ... This afternoon the campus police turned in their weekly police blotter to us, on time as always, but why didn't they let us know about the murder when it happened? I mean shit, their usual police blotter is full of garbage like juveniles igniting the iceplant at Student Apartments, it's good for a laugh but it's nothing we need before Tuesday afternoon. But murder! How come nobody saw fit to tell us? How come we didn't get a call from any of you? For God's sake, you **found** the sucker."

She paused for breath, and we reflected gravely on our failure to inform the press. Of course, we had assumed that the press would be informed without our assistance, and indeed this had been true of the **Banner.**

"So," said Mariah, "I want details. I want opinions. I want facts, I want conjectures, I want everything you can think of."

"Mariah," I said, "is this your typical interviewing style?"

"Are you kidding?" she said. "Of course it's not, but I know you guys, and I'm pissed off that we didn't have a chance to hop on this murder right away. Do you think I like staying up all night helping set type when usually I don't have to set any goddamn type at all? Tell me, how did you end up finding Gurney in the first place? I heard some wild story at the College Office about a dead hamster, but Linda and Kathryn were laughing too hard for me to make any sense out of it."

"We were having a wake," said Carolyn.

"Beast was dead," amplified Holly. "You remember Beast, don't you? She used to zip around the Hall in an exercise ball, and escape from her Habitrail and crawl through the radiator in the middle of the night."

"We used to have her crawl through paper towel rolls and scamper up and down our sleeves," said Tricia.

"Yeah, I seem to remember the hamster vaguely," said Mariah. "I remember the bit about the radiator, anyway. Wasn't she always getting put in the bathtub?"

"That was only when Carolyn wasn't home," said Evan. "We had to put her someplace she couldn't get out of."

"Hamsters are weird little critters," said Mariah. "So she was dead, and you were having a wake."

"Yeah, Carolyn put her in an Instant Lemonade can and we were going to bury her at the trash chute," said Tricia.

"Pretty fucking bizarre," said Mariah. "So who opened the door?"

"I did," said Holly. "There was a sign on it about it being full, but we didn't believe that for a minute, so I opened the door and there he was!"

"Gurney?"

"He was sitting there on the recyclable glass can looking like he'd dozed off or fainted or I don't know what," said Holly. "It was a shock. I didn't know **what** to do."

"There was no pulse," said Evan. "After a cursory examination it was pretty clear he was dead."

"Yeah, but how did he die?" said Mariah. "Nobody seems to know, or anyway they're not saying. Is there some kind of clue that we're supposed to suppress in order to catch the murderer, or are they just being dog-in-the-mangery about their info?"

"It's our understanding that he died of a blow to the neck," said Evan.

"Or, more precisely, to the throat," I said.

"It was the kind of injury a martial-arts student might inflict," said Evan, "except of course that we are also taught never to use this particular maneuver."

"Well, not unless someone is about to kill us," I said.

"So it's a really dangerous thing to do?" said Mariah.

"If you consider killing people to be dangerous," said Evan, "then yes, it's extremely dangerous. It is not a move one makes merely to cripple one's opponent."

"On the other hand," I said, "it's extremely easy to do. A person needn't be an advanced student. And once you've done it, there's not much anybody can do to save the person you've done it to."

"They won't die instantly, but there's no way of helping them," said Evan. "Not unless you've got medical people on the scene and can get the victim to the hospital immediately."

"That's awful!" burst out Holly.

"Horrible," said Mariah. "So do you think there's some reason that nobody's mentioned the means of death, or d'you think it's okay if we go ahead and put it in print?"

"Print," said Evan and Pauline.

"I don't know why you shouldn't," said Holly and Malcolm.

"Print it, print it," repeated Pauline.

"Okay, sounds good to me," said Mariah. "I just don't want to get in deep shit for screwing up police strategy. I mean, I'm big on freedom of the press and I'm not crazy about the cops, but I think the cops ought to catch murderers. If they spent more time on important stuff like this, they wouldn't get so uptight about garbage like whether my car registration's paid up."

This view of the law was hardly new, and I wondered whether Mariah was going to continue to expound her opinions or whether she had more questions for us.

"Is there anything else?" I inquired. "Some of us do have papers and other trivial interruptions to take care of."

Mariah looked at her notes, which sprawled illegibly all over the page. "Well, how did you all feel about finding the body?" she asked.

There was a brief silence.

"Surprised," said Malcolm.

"It was awful," said Holly firmly.

"Yeah, it was," agreed Tricia.

There was another silence. Mariah looked at us.

"That's a pretty weak showing," she said. "I'm supposed to quote you on that? '"**I was surprised,**" said Malcolm Dalton' and '"**It was awful,**" agreed two other witnesses'? Can't you do better than that? Get some pathos in there or something—makes you sound like you think dead bodies are on a par with the food in the dining room. '**When questioned about the yellow Baked Alaska served, students said "I was surprised" and "It was awful."**'"

"The yellow Baked Alaska *was* in exceedingly poor taste," said Evan.

"Don't distract me," said Mariah. "The yellow Baked Alaska was months ago and I don't give a shit about it, or maybe I should say a piss. Not that it was any worse than the black cookies they served at Halloween. Anyway, don't you have some kind of printable reaction to finding a dead body in the trash closet?"

"Printable?" said Carolyn.

"Yes, printable, what the hell do you think I want, off-the-record? Jesus, Carolyn, speak up! How did you feel when you saw Richard Gurney's dead body?"

Carolyn glanced at Holly, Tricia, and Pauline. "I felt sick. That's how I felt, I felt sick."

"Okay, I can tell I'm not going to get any stunning quotes out of any of you about finding the body," said Mariah. "D'you have any great theories on who did it? I don't have to print who, but it sounds good if somebody has an idea."

Again we looked at one another. We might speculate about Ferdinand or Theo or the other preceptors or about martial arts students in general, but did we have any suspects worthy of the name? It did not seem so.

"It must have been a person of considerable physical strength," said Evan, "as Gurney would hardly have been sitting on the trash can when he was killed."

"Yeah, and he wouldn't have been light," said Tricia. "I know I couldn't've carried him."

"Not fat," said Mariah, "but still a beefy dude."

"I do not like to speculate as to the sex of the murderer," continued Evan, "but I think that most people would be unable to move Richard Gurney **and** lift him onto the trash can."

"Absolutely," said Holly. "It's one thing to drag a person a short distance, but it's another matter entirely to lift a big limp body, especially if you're in a hurry."

"Maybe the murderer had an accomplice," said Carolyn, looking down at her peacock-blue Chinese shoes and twitching her toes.

"Ah, now we're getting somewhere," said Mariah happily. She scribbled at great speed, turning the pages in her notebook to accommodate her unintelligible handwriting and periodically poking me in the side with her elbow as a result. "An accomplice theory! I like it."

"Yes, but what good does it do us?" said Holly. "It just means two people to look for instead of one."

"And if you assume an accomplice, then the murderer no longer has to be particularly strong," observed Malcolm.

"Well, I think that even with an accomplice it'd get pretty tiring to lug Richard Gurney into the trash closet and stick him on top of one of those cans," said Holly. "It wouldn't be a job for a pair of weaklings."

"No," I said, "but what kind of person would help someone else dispose of a body?"

"They'd have to be awfully close friends," said Tricia dubiously.

"Well, unless they were both already incriminated in some way anyway," said Holly, equally dubiously.

"Would **you** help Carolyn dispose of a body?" asked Mariah.

10

There was a rather uncomfortable silence. Carolyn scowled and yanked at the loose threads at the end of her sleeve.

"I don't know," said Holly at last, "I guess it would depend on why she killed whoever it was. Besides, Carolyn wouldn't kill anyone, so it's pretty hard to imagine what I'd do if she **did.**"

"How do you know I wouldn't?" said Carolyn.

"Because you wouldn't," said Holly firmly. One gathered that she would deal summarily with any murderous ideas Carolyn might harbor.

"You don't know that," said Carolyn stubbornly. "For all you know, I'm a serial killer just waiting for the right moment to strike."

"You can't be a serial killer," scoffed Holly, "they're all men."

"Why should they all be men?" I said; perhaps the accumulating tension could be dissipated with a harmless discussion of serial killers. "Why shouldn't serial killers be women?"

"They never are," said Holly, "so it must be a genetic problem."

"That's rather broad," said Malcolm.

"Well, a Y chromosome problem, like hemophilia."

"You mean X," I said. "Sex-linked genetic diseases are passed through the mother, who doesn't get the disease because she has a second X chromosome to offset the defective one." I was rather proud of myself for being able to remember this bit of biology.

"The second X chromosome doesn't offset the defective one," asserted Evan, "it's a matter of whether the gene in question is dominant or recessive."

"Maybe serial killers have an extra Y chromosome," said Carolyn; "men who do are more violent."

"You can't have an extra chromosome," said Holly. "That's impossible."

"No it's not," said Carolyn, "they say lots of violent criminals have an extra Y. I forget what they call it, it's somebody or other's syndrome."

"Hold it, hold it," exclaimed Mariah, "I came here to interview you, not to get some kind of half-assed genetics lecture about fucking serial killers. Jesus."

"I would not dream of discussing the notion of sexual relations with serial killers," said Evan with considerable disapproval.

"Oh, Jesus. Let's not go into that, okay? I don't want to know about genetics, and I don't want to know about serial killers, 'cause I'll be deeply amazed if a serial killer did in Richard Gurney. As it now stands, a person or persons unknown killed and moved him, and I've got a big long article to write **and** probably help typeset, and the last goddamn thing I want to hear about is genetic problems among serial killers. Now, do any of you have any further intelligent remarks to make before I get out of here and go write my article? Like, can I use your names in it or are you going to be tiresome about that?"

Mariah, I thought, was a rather naïvely over-scrupulous journalist. A professional reporter would have waited for us to insist on confidentiality, or said you couldn't go off the record after the fact, not offered silence to us on a silver platter.

"I don't know about everyone else," I said, "but my own preference would be for there to be as little mention of our names as possible. You could say things like 'one of the students who discovered the body,' and so on."

"I don't care if you use my name," said Tricia. "I don't think anybody's going to come after me."

"Wait," said Holly, "I think if any of us're going to be mentioned, we should all be. And we don't know whether anybody might come after us or not, so I don't think any of us should be. Okay?"

This made a certain amount of sense, so it did not take us long to agree that none of us should be mentioned. When these formalities had been concluded, Mariah slapped shut her notebook, stuck her pen in the wire spiral, and, hurriedly thanking us for our time, removed herself to write.

"This better not take me all night," she said gloomily. "I've still got a half-finished article on the Lina Troyer tenure question to do, too."

"If I hear another word about Lina Troyer's tenure," said Holly, "I'll puke. If she weren't a

Marxist and a lesbian, no one would pay any attention to her tenure."

Mariah stuck her head back in the door. "Maybe," she said, "but don't you think it's important?"

Then she vanished, for good or for ill, and the rest of us remained in the lounge for a few moments, somewhat dazed by the energy—if not the exactitude—of her questioning. After a moment, Holly said "I don't care how important Lina Troyer's tenure is, I'm too **tired** to care. I've got too many rehearsals to care. Maybe I'll care about it tomorrow and maybe I won't. Mariah really gets on my nerves sometimes."

There was no answer to this. Tricia said "Are you and Carolyn rehearsing again tonight?"

"No, for once," said Holly; "we already did this afternoon." She glanced at Carolyn. "How's Seneca?"

"Nasty. Give me Euripides any day."

There was a knock on the door, and two honorary Hall members, Dave and Myron, entered.

"Anyone wanna play Euchre?" said Myron, pulling out his usual grimy deck from the back pocket of his usual sagging double-knits. Myron's mental and emotional world would probably collapse if he were prevented from playing Euchre on a regular basis.

"Sure," said Evan. Holly and Carolyn pried themselves from the sofa and stood up.

"How about you, Carolyn?" asked Myron.

"No thanks," said Carolyn. She shuddered slightly.

"We've got work to do," said Holly, and they and Tricia and Pauline slipped out the door. Myron is not overly popular with the female residents of the Hall, or with women in general.

"I'll play a game or two," I said, though I too had work to do.

We rearranged ourselves to positions suitable to the playing of cards; Myron began to shuffle.

"I hear you found Richard Gurney," said Dave.

"Word travels fast," I said.

"Not very, actually," said Dave with a grin. "It must have been a surprise!"

I was pleased to hear that we weren't the only ones to call our discovery "surprising." "It was," I admitted.

"I wonder if anyone's told his girlfriend?"

"Girlfriend?" I said.

"Richard Gurney had a **girlfriend?**" said Evan.

The idea did indeed seem strange. How could Richard Gurney have had a girlfriend without our knowing about it? True, there were many things we did not know about him, but we had not expected a girlfriend to be one of them.

"Don't you remember that girl from Utah?" said Dave. "Blonde and sort of cute? Wore halter tops all the time?"

"Oh, her ... But didn't she go back to Utah? She couldn't've been too interested in him if she went back to Utah."

"Maybe not, but she might like to know that he's dead," said Dave. "I wonder if anyone has her address."

"I don't think she fit in very well here," said Evan. "Apparently she underwent a religious conversion and decided that her place was in the home."

"I suppose she was a Mormon to begin with," said Dave.

"Surely there aren't any Mormons here," I said; "don't they all go to BYU and learn to hoard food and put skirts on immodest detergent bottles?"

We considered this notion with distaste, and then Myron, a bit slow as usual to get the gist of events in the world outside his lab, asked who Richard Gurney was and what had happened to him, and how he had met the girl from Utah. I suspected he really hoped to learn how Gurney had become a success with women.

None of this was the sort of thing that the rest of us were very interested in explaining from A to Z, and consequently the conversation rapidly went to other topics.

Wednesday morning marked the distribution of **Fun Times,** the weekly entertainment paper, a ridiculous but often amusing tabloid that has few if any pretensions to journalism. Apart from its calendar, it boasts a variety of features: articles about anyone and anything appearing in town; discussions of local clubs and their owners and feuds between same; cartoons of a primarily local origin; a gossip column; an advice column; a horoscope column; a large section of Personal classifieds; and a great deal of other material, none of which could really be called news. Piles of this remarkable publication are always left outside the dining room, so that Wednesday lunch is primarily notable for the number of people who eat with their faces in the midst of two-color printing.

I did not bother to pick up a copy of **Fun Times** as I made my way into the dining room on this particular Wednesday, but the Gang of Four were, predictably, deeply immersed.

"Look, Carolyn," Tricia was saying, "Archie Fisher's going to be in town in a couple of weeks!"

Carolyn looked up from the horoscopes, which she was dipping into her lasagna. "How much're tickets?" she inquired.

"Eight bucks at the door, seven-fifty advance. Wanna go?"

I gathered that Archie Fisher was a Scottish folk singer, and put down my tray next to Holly's.

"What's your sign, Keith?" asked Carolyn.

"Gemini," I said.

"Oh good, that's what I thought," she re-marked, and read:

> You'll discover something unset-tling if you keep digging around in the dirt, but maybe you just like muckraking. Watch your step if you don't want to hurt people. It helps to sweat a lot and never mind the deodorant. Remember, God is a ma-chine that loves you ...

"It doesn't say any of that," I said. "You're mak-ing that up."

"No way, it's right here." She pointed at the horoscopes, and I observed that it was indeed.

"What's yours?" I said, and read:

> Your tongue surprises you with some malevolent slips. All your best slang this week originates in mis-

taken identities and coincidental substitutions. You're almost obligated to sublimate your planetary energies into an exploration of the unconscious. Keep the ma out of madonna for now.

"Bizarre as usual," I said, glancing at the adjoining headlines, which said: "Learn to Dowse" and "Half of all widows have sensed the presence of their dead husbands at home, according to a university study."

"But Keith," said Holly, "as far as I can tell, the only mention they make of Richard Gurney is in that stupid Hal Hollis column. Look."

She turned the page, and again I looked.

Don Fontanella and the Raging Kumquats are coming to the Asterisk Friday night, and if you haven't seen 'em before, now's the time to be sure and catch this red-hot group. Believe me, they've got a wild show.

I grimaced and continued.

But if you like your music a little more romantic, Toni and the Turtles are performing nightly at the Inn, where they've been deservedly successful for the last five seasons. I hear Toni's got a new set of performance gowns designed by local talent Sandy Bergstrom. Sandy's been working real hard down at Campostello Costumes making some incredible items like a giant green caterpillar and some that are still top-secret until Halloween, but ...

I turned away in disgust. Toni and the Turtles? Local talent Sandy Bergstrom? "Spare me," I said.

"Spare me this drivel about giant caterpillars and Toni the Turtle."

"Not that shit," said Holly. She stuck her finger in the middle of the type. "Further down."

I removed her finger and read Hollis' further tiresome gabbling until I reached **"I've been hearing some nasty rumors about something happening up on campus, but no one will confirm anything. Stay tuned for more."**

"Is that all he says?"

"All," said Holly.

"He could mean anything from Gilbert and Lainey dancing nude at parties to gossip about Lina Troyer's love life."

"No, he means Richard Gurney being murdered," said Holly.

"You don't know that," I said, and returned at last to my lasagna. After being fanned by all of those newspapers, it had become a trifle cold, but it was still one of the kitchen's better offerings. I had little attention to spare for the Gang of Four's recitations from the Personals column, which included: "Raven-haired priestess, 29, seeks high priest for nocturnal erotic worship"; "Sexy ex-surfer, 36, seeks same for shared fun, occasional dinners"; "Man with six toes and beautiful smile, I lost your number"; and "Sarolta, please call before I get frantic!" I had a class to get to, and I would always be able to read this trivia later, when Carolyn had cut out the best of it and put it on her door.

11

The martial-arts class was as usual that night, though I noticed that Zoe Vogel was absent. No doubt she was still suffering from that nasty-looking flu.

Back at the Hall, Holly met us again with a newspaper.

"Keith, there's finally something worth reading about Richard Gurney!" she exclaimed.

"Holly," I said, "You give me a strange feeling of dejà-vu the way you keep coming at me with newspapers these days. Why do you feel this need to burden me with the outpourings of the press?"

"Keith, sometimes I just don't understand you," she said, stamping her foot. "There's all kinds of valuable information in the newspaper, or at least there **ought** to be. This time there's finally some in-depth reporting on the murder; Mariah got in her article."

"Let me see," said Evan. She handed him the paper and he began to peruse it.

"Just because Mariah happened to interview us doesn't mean we're going to learn anything from her article," I said. "What's the rush? It's only a secondary source—it's probably full of hearsay and mistakes."

Holly threw up her hands and waved them vigorously about as if she expected an airplane to land in front of her. "Historiographers!" she groaned.

"**We** are a primary source," I said; "Mariah's article is a secondary source. And," I added, recalling a rather appropriate quotation from Voltaire, "'In the case of news, we should always wait for the sacrament of confirmation.'"

Holly paid no attention to Voltaire, perhaps thinking that this was merely some silly remark of my own. "We," she said, "are a primary source not in possession of all the facts; we are a primary source that might learn something from the newspapers."

I conceded this. Perhaps it was my awareness that Holly and the rest of the Gang of Four were withholding information from me that inclined me to be so uninterested in her newspaper articles.

"It's not a bad article," remarked Evan. "Mariah seems to have done her research."

"I didn't notice any inaccuracies," said Holly. "That's always a good sign."

"She seems to have a talent for ferreting things out," Evan went on.

Holly began to giggle. "She looks more like an elephant seal than a ferret!"

"Not around the nose," I said, taking the paper from Evan. "And a good thing, too. It's one thing to be fat, but to have a nose like an elephant seal ..."

Mariah is really not all **that** fat. No doubt some people would merely call her well-upholstered, though her behavior has little in common with the average chair or sofa. However, musing that none of this was in fact germane, I began to read the article. It was indeed not a bad one. Mariah seemed to have interviewed a good many people—in addition to us, she had interviewed the College secretaries, the police, someone at the Health Center, and a sprinkling of random students.

Her primary thrust seemed to be that the Administration was keeping information from the students to a degree that amounted to cover-up. She asserted that Gurney had been murdered Saturday night by a person or persons unknown, and that not only was this person still at large endangering the community, but that the College had not seen fit to announce any of this until Tuesday night. She demanded, on behalf of the population at large, to know why this information had been withheld.

I paused to consider this. Certainly I knew of no reason for the College to have delayed its announcement so long.

"Maybe she's right about this cover-up theory," I said. "Maybe we should reconsider Ferdinand and Theo and the rest of the staff."

"We never considered them very thoroughly to begin with," said Evan. "It would be wise to make a list and go through it in a logical way."

"A list of suspects!" said Holly. "That's exactly what we need!" She ran into her room for paper and pencil, and on her return was joined by Carolyn, wrapped in a long blue chenille bathrobe and drinking tequila-and-lemonade.

"Who're the suspects?" asked Carolyn.

"If the College is doing a cover-up," I said, "it stands to reason that the murderer is probably a staff member."

"You don't think they're just trying to avoid scandal?"

"What do you mean, scandal?" I said. "There's always some kind of scandal going on around here, conventionally speaking. We're a scandalous college. We are not Oral Roberts University or a girls' finishing school."

"Don't be silly, Keith," said Holly. "Of course we aren't either of those things, but that doesn't mean the Administration has no regard for appearances."

"Having a regard for appearances is not the same thing as covering up a murder for three days," I said. "Maybe the delay isn't a cover-up, but I'll bet it is."

"Well, we're not arguing with the possibility," said Holly.

"So," said Carolyn, pulling herself out of her mug of tequila again, "who are the suspects?"

"Ferdinand for one," said Evan.

"Theo."

"The rest of the preceptors."

"Wait, we need to list the preceptors separately," said Holly. "Who are they all again?"

"Margo," said Carolyn. "And Daryl Green."

"Nina," said Evan.

"Bob and Diana," I said.

"I think that's all," said Holly.

"I **hope** that's all," I said. "The idea of four hundred suspects is rather daunting."

"Four hundred?" said Carolyn.

"Well, isn't that how many people there are in this college, give or take a few?"

"Hey, the college directory ought to list all the preceptors and RAs," said Holly. "Do we still have ours?"

She went over to the phone, where at the beginning of each year these rather short-lived dittoes are stapled along with the list of emergency numbers that had come in so handy when we had discovered Richard Gurney. To all of our surprise, the directory was still in place, and we had succeeded in listing all the preceptors correctly from memory. Now, spurning memory, we listed the RAs.

"Yuck," said Carolyn. "Suspects all over the place, and I'll bet none of them did it. Besides, if there's a cover-up, then it wasn't an RA. They wouldn't do a cover-up on an RA any faster than on any other student."

"True," said Evan, "but we need to list them anyway in order to interview them."

"Wouldn't we need only Gurney's RAs?" said Carolyn.

"I'll put a star next to them," said Holly. We examined her handiwork and found it clear enough.

"I suppose we should list Relief Proctor Sally," remarked Evan.

"**Sally!**" said Carolyn in some distress.

"She's a staff member and she was in the area," he reminded her.

"Yeah, but really!"

"Well, she'd better go on the list just to be thorough," said Holly. "That way we can always check her off as soon as we eliminate her for sure."

"I guess it makes sense," said Carolyn, "but this idea of listing everybody under the sun as a suspect is kind of unnerving. We could be listing ourselves at this rate." She pulled her knees up under her chin, wrapping the blue chenille bathrobe around them with unnecessary force, and looked unhappy.

"We **don't** need to list ourselves," said Holly briskly, giving her a look, "because we know where we all were."

"No we don't," rejoined Carolyn, "not all day we don't. We don't know what time he was killed, so we don't have any alibis."

Evan and I glanced at each other. Why was she harping on this?

"I don't have an alibi," she went on. "I could have killed him."

"No you could not," said Evan.

"I could too," said Carolyn.

"Well, you didn't," said Holly.

"I might've," insisted Carolyn.

"I wish," said Evan, "that you would stop aggrandizing yourself in this really perverse way. We all know that you did not kill Richard Gurney, and your ridiculous assertions only waste time and distract us from more tenable theories."

Both Carolyn and Holly glared at him.

"The important thing right now," I said hastily, "is to interview the various preceptors and RAs. I will be happy to talk to Theo Roth, and we can all talk to Relief Proctor Sally when she comes on; do any of you have preferences regarding the others?"

They examined the list.

"It's hard to interview total strangers," said Carolyn.

Holly and Evan initialed the persons they knew well enough to interview, and I observed that this came to a satisfactory number.

The next morning I duly made my way to Theo Roth's office, a large and surprisingly sunny room on the first floor of Holland House, adorned by an abstract oil in red and blue, a slightly torn travel poster depicting the Swiss Alps, and large diagrams of the two dorms with all our names penciled in the appropriate boxes. As I opened the door, a pudgy, dark-haired woman with a very discontented expression pushed through, nearly crashing into me. Theo looked up from the papers on his desk.

"Hey, Keith," he said pleasantly, "what can I do for you? I hope you don't want to move, I'm tired of dealing with that today."

I expressed my continuing contentment with my abode. "Although, mind you, we still have some problems with the damp. Holly found another mushroom growing out of her carpet last week, so we wondered if there was any truth to the rumor that the University gets an insurance break on buildings that can be considered waterlogged."

Theo covered his face and groaned. "I don't want to hear any more about that either!" he said. "God, what a thankless job. Did you see that girl who left just as you were coming in?"

"Yes," I said.

"Do you know her?"

"No," I admitted.

Theo allowed himself a smile. "Count your blessings," he said. "Of the several banes of my existence, Rhoda Bortz could be considered one of the worst."

"Rhoda Bortz?" I asked. It seemed as though I had heard that name recently, though I could not think when. "Who's she? What does she want?"

"What doesn't she want?" exclaimed Theo. "I know I shouldn't be talking about one student to another, but that Rhoda is really an effing pain. I wish she'd move downtown. She lives on the Girls' Hall because she's such a fucking virgin, but it seems like she can't go a week without bitching about something or other on her Hall."

"I think I **have** heard of her," I said. "I seem to remember hearing that at one of Richard Gurney's sherry parties she spent the whole time being nasty to Zoe Vogel."

"Oh God," said Theo, "don't even mention those names to me. Talk about more banes of my meagre existence ... Why did I ever hire that bozo Gurney? What planet was I on? How could I have been so stupid?"

"You couldn't have known he was going to be murdered," I said, wondering whether, on the contrary, Theo **had** known.

"No, of course not," he said, "but that's neither here nor there. If I hadn't hired him, either he'd still be alive and kicking or he'd be dead somewhere else, and either way I wouldn't have to think about him. As it is, now I'm stuck with all the questions, and Ferdinand is looking at me like he thinks I was out of my mind to hire the guy, which of course I feel like I was."

"Did you have any problems with Gurney before he got killed?" I asked.

"Oh—" Theo waved his hand across the desk—"nothing **really** to speak of. But you know what he was like. He seemed like an okay guy at first, and I suppose he was okay in his way, but people never really liked him. You know, some preceptors are really popular and really keep an eye on things, some are just sort of okay, and some end up being kind of marginal. Richard was one of the marginal guys."

"There must've been something worse than marginal about him for him to get murdered," I said.

"Maybe," said Theo, "but not necessarily. People get murdered all the time just because they were in the wrong place at the wrong time."

"True," I said, "but not around here. Isn't it more likely that Gurney was supposed to get killed than that Damson House is a dangerous place to be?"

"Well, I guess I'd rather that that was the case; that wouldn't be nearly so hard to deal with," said Theo. "But either way it still comes under the heading of Big Problems for the Housing Co-ordinator. Either I went and hired someone who got himself murdered, or else I've totally missed hearing about some kind of really bad scene going on here."

"True," I said. "But which do you think was more likely?"

"Well, I can't be sure," said Theo. "The whole thing was so unexpected. Besides, if he did something to get himself killed, that in itself suggests dangerous goings-on in general. For instance, I don't pay much attention to ordinary recreational drug use. I'd go out of my mind if I tried, and I'd only lose people's confidence. People go away to school and either they keep taking the same things they took at home, or they make a point of finding what they couldn't get at home. Or, of course, they just aren't interested. And so, as long as nobody gets hurt or screws up their studies, I figure it's none of my business. I mean, I can't let people grow pot plants in their rooms, but you know what I mean. But suppose it turned out that there was something more serious going on that I wasn't aware of, you know, like some kind of heavy drug dealing, not just people selling some buds here and some mushrooms there. You know what I mean?"

"Yes." I didn't think it sounded very likely, but it was certainly a possibility. At least it offered the prospect of a motive, and up to now we had not done very well in thinking up likely motives. I looked at Theo. He was sitting with his feet up on the desk, tilted back in his chair, just as he usually was. "Do you have any idea who might be the murderer?" I inquired.

But before Theo could say more than "Oy, what a question!" the door opened.

12

"I hope I'm not interrupting," said a voice. Turning my head, I recognized a woman I had occasionally seen talking to Tricia, Renee Gibeau.

"Nah," said Theo, "do we really look like we're immersed in actual work? We're just shooting the breeze about life and death, especially death. Pull up a chair."

Renee complied and sat down. She looked extremely self-contained, her long dark hair hanging smoothly down her back, her hands clasped in her lap, her Levi's neither new nor torn, and her ankles neatly crossed above her black Chinese shoes.

"What can I do for you?" said Theo, bringing his chair and feet back to the floor and leaning forward on his elbows atop the month-at-a-glance disposable desk blotter.

"Well," said Renee judiciously, "actually it's for my roommate."

"Who is ..."

"Zoe Vogel."

There was a very slight pause, and then Theo said "Oh! So you're Zoe's roommate. Right. I don't know how I could've forgotten that. I suppose she still wants to get out of her housing contract."

"Yes," said Renee.

"You know, she's already talked to me about it a couple of times," said Theo. "If she'd just wait till the end of the quarter, it'd all be easy. I don't know why she's so hot to break her housing contract in the middle like this, it's just stupid."

"Maybe," said Renee, "but she really wants to get out of the dorms. Can't you just let her go? She's never here anyway. She's got a place downtown she can move into, and lately she's been really depressed. She's under a lot of stress."

"It seems to me that moving is pretty stressful in and of itself," said Theo. "Why can't she wait and do it at Spring Break?"

"She wants to move now," reiterated Renee, "and it's getting really hard to live with her. I mean, I like her okay as a person, and she's not around a lot, but she's still hard to live with. It's like I get depressed every time I walk into the room, just because she's depressed. It makes me feel funny."

"Hmm," said Theo, probably because there was not much else to be said to this.

"I wish you'd let her move," said Renee. "We'd both really appreciate it."

"Well, I'll think about it," said Theo. "I don't want to make any promises yet though."

Renee stood up. "Okay," she said. "I'll tell Zoe."

I stood up as well; it didn't seem as though I was going to get much more information out of Theo, and I was a little worried about Zoe.

"How's Zoe's flu?" I asked Renee as we left the office.

"Flu?" said Renee. She looked puzzled.

"Doesn't she have the flu? She left class sick on Monday and didn't come at all Wednesday, so I figured she had that new Asian flu." It occurred to me that all new flu viruses seemed to come from Asia these days; why was it that no one ever got anything called the Hungarian Flu, or the Brazilian Flu, or the Australian Flu, or the Chicago Flu?

"I don't think she exactly had the flu," said Renee slowly, "unless she just had a stomach bug Monday night. But I don't see much of Zoe. She spends all her time downtown at Bronwen Bay Laurel's house."

"I thought she was involved with Lina Troyer," I said.

Renee blushed slightly. "Nobody's supposed to know that," she said severely.

"No, but everyone does."

"Maybe, but don't go around telling people. Zoe's got enough problems."

"Why, what problems has Zoe got besides Lina Troyer and getting out of her housing contract? And why's she so anxious to get out of her housing contract? Theo's right about it being silly to leave in the middle of the quarter."

"She wants to get out of her housing contract because Bronwen's her best friend and there's a room open in Bronwen's house right now. She's sick of living in the dorms and the house is only gay women."

"So she sent you to get on Theo's case about it?"

Renee looked quite inscrutable. "Sort of. I don't know why you care."

"Well, Zoe's a friend of mine," I said. "We've taken a lot of classes together and all that."

"Well, then ask **her** about it. I'm only her room-mate." Renee looked at me for a second and then, muttering "See ya," walked away.

I was mildly peeved. It was true that Zoe and I were friends, but I had more immediate concerns than her housing contract and her affair with Lina Troyer. For instance, the meeting I was expected to have with my advisor in ten minutes.

❦

"Well," Liz was saying to an audience of Tricia, Pauline, and Carolyn as I brought my tray to our usual table, "it was there by about 9:30, because that's about when I went to clean Hemingway's cage in the maid's closet, only luckily I saw the sign first so I went upstairs."

Hemingway was Liz's rabbit, a fat buck of the English Spot breed.

"Why up?" said Carolyn.

"Well, I didn't think the trash'd be full another floor up," said Liz, "and of course it wasn't, so I washed out Hemingway's cage and put in fresh newspapers, and in the meantime he had jumped onto my bed and peed on my pillow."

"Naughty bunny," said Tricia fondly.

"Yes, it was very bad of him," agreed Liz. "I don't know what more I can do to make him stop; he knows he's not supposed to do that."

I sat down with my tray. "So the sign was up by 9:30," I said.

Tricia and Pauline looked irritably at me. "Yes," said Tricia.

This was becoming tiresome. What had I done to fall from grace? Occasionally Tricia and I had our tiffs, but I was not accustomed to being excluded from important counsels.

"I'm pretty sure it was around then," said Liz, "because I wanted to get Hemingway's cage done and get on over to that party in Holland House."

"Naughty bun-bun," said Tricia again.

"He only does it to get attention," said Liz.

"You should bring him over to visit Aunt Tricia more often," said the animal's besotted relative. "He never pees in my room; he's always very well-behaved."

"He's a lot more fun than Beast was," agreed Carolyn. "He likes to be petted, anyway, and he likes it when I chew on his ears."

"He's a good bunny," said Tricia.

"Yes, he is," said Liz. "I just wish I could get him to stop peeing."

"Send him to obedience school!" said Tricia as Holly joined us.

"Send who to obedience school," said Holly, "Keith?"

"I resent that remark," I said.

"Hemingway, of course," said Tricia.

"Oh," said Holly. It was clear that she was not deeply interested in Hemingway or his misdemeanors. "Well, I went and talked to Bob and Diana this morning," she said.

"Who?" asked Pauline.

"You know, the married preceptors," said Holly impatiently. "I went to ask them what they thought about Richard Gurney."

"Oh!" said Pauline.

"What'd they say?" I asked.

"Not a whole lot," said Holly. "They were very guarded. They invited me in for a cup of tea, and I sat on their spiffy new flowered sofa asking them what they thought of him and they sat there in their nice new rattan chairs asking me if I wanted sugar in my tea and saying that they didn't really know him all that well, that they only really saw him at preceptor meetings."

"The question that springs to mind, of course," I said, "is whether this is true or just their way of avoiding the issue."

"Probably both," said Holly. "They didn't seem like his type—you know, they're so genteel and Nice Young People Who Got Married. They seem like the kind of people who never do anything that might be in bad taste."

"I wonder what they're doing here?" said Carolyn. "They must feel like they landed on the wrong planet."

"Actually they're really nice," said Pauline, to my surprise.

"Maybe they're anthropologists studying us," Carolyn went on.

"They said," said Holly, "that occasionally at meetings Gurney would complain that none of his Halls ever wanted to follow through on any of his ideas, and that the turnout for his sherry parties was abysmal."

"We knew that," said Tricia. "Hey Holly, according to Liz the sign on the trash chute was up by about 9:30."

"Really," said Holly. "Then a lot of people could've opened that door and seen him before we did."

"Yeah," said Carolyn. "We were pretty late. I wonder who saw him there and didn't say anything?"

"I don't think very many could've," said Liz. "I think most people would've called the police the minute they found a body."

"But it's not so important who saw the body as who put it there," continued Holly. "Half-past nine's a strange time to be moving bodies, or eight, or seven—anytime in the evening you'd expect people to come wandering by. I mean, people are always going up and down the stairs."

"True," I said, giving up on my sandwich.

"What about dinner-time?" said Carolyn.

"Maybe," said Tricia. "It'd still be risky, though."

"It'd be risky anytime," said Holly. "There's no getting around that."

Malcolm joined us, settling an enormous pile of library books beside a modest tray. "Killing people is always risky. Best to indulge in the wee hours of the morning."

"Two or three A.M. would be the best time to move a body," agreed Holly.

"Best, maybe, but how convenient?" I said.

"Well, if you want convenience ..." said Tricia.

"How convenient is it to kill somebody?" said Liz.

"Death is generally inconvenient," remarked Carolyn, "especially to the dead person."

"Not for suicides," said Pauline.

"Suicides are beside the point," said Holly over Tricia and Carolyn's "By the sewer I lived, by the sewer I died, they said it was murder—but it was sewercide!"

"The person who killed Gurney probably couldn't wait very long to dispose of the body," I said. "Not knowing whether the act was premeditated, it's hard to say whether putting the body in the trash represented insult or expediency."

"Or whether the murderer killed Gurney in his room—the murderer's room, I mean—" said Liz, "and had to get the body out of the way before his roommate came back."

"That's a thought," I agreed. All of us, even Liz, were so privileged as to live in singles, but of course this was not true of most people in the dorm. Tricia and Pauline began to speculate how long one might endure a corpse in one's bedroom before it began either to smell or to be noticed by visitors—

"Not very long in **my** room," said Tricia, "but I don't know about **yours,** Pauline, I think somebody could hide a body in your room for at least a week before anyone could tell the difference. And everyone would know right away if Keith or Holly had a body in one of their rooms, because so many people go in and out."

I did not think that this was quite accurate, as people spend more time sitting in my doorway than they do actually in my room, but in essence she was correct.

"And Evan wouldn't be able to stand the smell," said Tricia.

"Unless of course he happened to like that kind of thing, which is always possible," said Carolyn.

"Ugh!" said Holly.

"Some people do," said Carolyn.

"Not very many, I hope!" said Tricia.

"I bet Seneca was one," said Carolyn.

"Oh, Seneca," said Holly aggrievedly, "I wish I'd never heard of him. Whose class do you have to write that for, anyway?"

"Calvin Shaw's. He's such a pervert, he likes that kind of thing."

"Maybe **he** killed Richard Gurney," suggested Tricia gaily.

"Nah, he just gets off on sicko plays," said Carolyn. "He's too wimpy to kill anyone in hand-to-hand combat. I bet you I'll do really well in his class if I pick a gross enough scene to do for my final project. He'd love it if I did Jocasta stabbing herself in the womb ... God, I hate required classes!"

Agreeing in this last, we all sighed, and forcibly changed the subject.

13

On our way back to our rooms after lunch, I tried to total up the results of our investigations to date. We had questioned Steve Madison, the College secretaries, Theo Roth, and Preceptors Bob and Diana; and even before we reached the dormitory stairs, it was already painfully clear to me that in all of these encounters we had come up with approximately nothing. Liz had supplied the information that the sign was in place by 9:30, but apart from that, what had we learned? Steve had provided us with nothing; Kathy and Linda were no more knowledgeable than we; Theo was worried about the effect the murder would have on his job; and Bob and Diana were bland and useless.

I realized that it had been nearly a week since the murder and we had only succeeded in questioning six people. Really, this was appalling! What sort of detectives were we, that after finding a body on Saturday night we had failed to interview more than six people by Thursday lunch? True, we had classes, and rehearsals, and papers, and homework, but there were also seven of us, eight if you counted Liz. What had we been doing? Reading newspapers?

I tried to think what I had been doing over the last several days, and could only come up with a blur of history seminars punctuated by meals, studying, sleep, and attempts at detection. Perhaps being a student took more of my time than I had previously realized. Perhaps it was not surprising that the police, who are paid to spend their hours preventing and solving crimes, catch more murderers than do average citizens.

Still, the police had evidently not yet come to any stunning solutions yet, which left the field open for amateurs like us.

"Hey," I said as I unlocked my door, "is anyone questioning any suspects this afternoon?"

"Are you kidding?" said Tricia. "I have a three-hour drawing class and I'm already late! Oh gosh, where'd I put my pad? Pauline, did I leave my big sketch pad in your room?"

"How should I know?"

"Jeez ... Oh, never mind, I found it under my bed. I guess I put it there to get it out of the way when I vacuumed this morning."

"I questioned Bob and Diana this morning and that was **boring,**" said Holly shortly. "I don't think any of the preceptors know anything. I don't know why we have preceptors anyway, unless it's to make freshmen feel secure."

"Why should freshmen need to feel secure?" said Carolyn. "I never did when I was a freshman; I was too busy to worry about dumb things like whether I felt secure."

"Secure!" giggled Tricia, emerging with her sketch pad. "I wonder how many freshmen are on the phone to mom and dad right now saying they don't feel secure."

"'Mommy, I'm scared,'" said Pauline, mimicking a childish voice, "'I wanna go home.'"

"Freshmen and their needs are beside the point," I said, feeling that I had heard enough of this nonsense. "Someone ought to interview Ferdinand, and I have a class this afternoon."

"I'm not interviewing Ferdinand," said Tricia.

"Me neither," said Carolyn and Pauline, Carolyn adding "I hate talking to people I don't know very well."

"Excuses!" exclaimed Holly. "Excuses, excuses!"

"Well, I have to get off to that stupid Calvin Shaw class, anyway," said Carolyn. "I don't know why I always end up with at least one **tedious** class, and it's always **required.**"

"Nobody forced you to take his stupid class and write gory papers about Seneca," said Holly. "You could've petitioned your way out and fulfilled the requirement with something else."

"I thought it might turn out to be a good class," said Carolyn glumly. "I mean, early drama isn't intrinsically boring. But the class is totally dead. Besides, maybe I don't have good translations or something, but I thought the **Agamemnon** and the **Poetics** were dull, and I wish the Romans had never existed."

"Did you finish your paper yet?" inquired Tricia.

"Yes, finally!" said Carolyn, giving her backpack a thump. "I'm disposing of it the minute I get to class."

"Well, speaking of class," said Tricia, "I have **got** to go."

This being in fact the case with all of us, we grabbed books, notebooks, pens, and backpacks as needed, locked our doors, and headed towards the stairs.

But no sooner had we set foot outside our own Hall and onto the industrial-quality tile whose appearance so offends the eye with its ground-in dirt and McCarthy-era pattern of black streaks on off-white, than a pair of policemen erupted from the stairwell.

They were, in fact, the same policemen whom we had had the privilege to meet some days back.

A little uncertain whether to step forward and greet them, or whether to retreat and avoid annoying them, we hesitated a second. Then Pauline stepped forth, sketch pad in hand, and hailed them.

"Officer Denny!" she exclaimed, in tones more suited to the return of a lost loved one than to a member of the police force whose acquaintance had been made over a dead body. She rushed towards Officer Denny, effectively halting his progress, and astonishing all concerned. Holly, Carolyn, and I gaped, especially when Tricia followed her example and also greeted him with cries of "Officer Denny!"

"Is everything all right?" Tricia demanded, before he or anyone else could speak. "I mean, no one else's been murdered, have they?"

"No, no, nobody else's been murdered," said Officer Denny with a glance at his colleague. Officer Morales said nothing.

"That's good!" said Pauline sagely. "Have you found the murderer yet?"

"Yeah," chorused Tricia, "have you got him yet?"

Officers Denny and Morales looked at each other, perhaps in commiseration at being stuck with such a hyperactive and largely white group of students.

"No, I'm afraid we haven't caught him yet," said Officer Denny. "Have you got something to tell us?"

"No," said Pauline, while Tricia said "Rats! I was hoping you'd have it all figured out by this time. Have you gotten all those fingerprints analyzed yet?"

Officer Denny grinned. Apparently his business was not of any great urgency; in fact, it was entirely possible that the police had returned in the hopes of seeing **us** again, in which case they had done rather well.

"Well, let's say that none of the fingerprints have ID'd with any known criminals," he said. "Most likely they're all student fingerprints. I don't suppose anyone cleans that door too often—we had more prints off it than Carter's got pills."

"Rats," said Tricia again. "Oh well, we could've guessed he wasn't murdered by some famous criminal. But did you find anything else interesting?" Her desire to get to class seemed to have evaporated, but then, so had everyone else's.

"Was there anything left on the body to identify the killer?" asked Holly with considerable interest. "Did he draw any blood in the struggle?"

"Blood, guts, and blueberry stains!" chanted Carolyn in a whisper, referring perhaps to some book or incident from her childhood.

"No blood or anything like that," said Officer Denny, smiling—evidently he felt that they might as well humor us—"but I don't see any harm in telling you that the forensic examiners have found **lint** adhering to the victim's clothes. Looks like he might've been carried in a blanket, but there weren't corresponding particles on the floor." He scratched his large and balding head, in a manner that suggested he was the original model for thoughtful older head-scratching policemen.

"You think someone carried him in a blanket and then took it back home with them?" said Tricia. "Eyyeww, that's disgusting!"

"Is that what you're here for now?" said Holly.

Officer Denny allowed a small silence during which we all contemplated the notion of a general search. I was pretty certain that none of us had anything very illegal in our possession—after all, the police would not haul Tricia and Pauline down to the station for owning bootleg Patti Smith LPs—but very likely much of the rest of the college would be loath to display their gro-lites, roach clips, stash-bags, and hallucinogenic cacti.

"Are you going to search the whole dorm?" asked Tricia.

"Do you think we should?" inquired Officer Denny.

"It seems kind of difficult to search a whole dorm," said Tricia dubiously.

"You'd have to have a search warrant for that anyway," said Holly.

"Well, no need to worry about that yet, because we're just here to interview a young woman who thinks she noticed something suspicious."

⊰⊱ ·◆· ⊰⊱

I need hardly describe the excitement that greeted this pronouncement.

"Suspicious?" said Pauline.

"A witness?" cried Tricia.

"Amazing!" said Carolyn.

"A clue!" exclaimed Holly.

"Who is the young woman in question?" I inquired.

Officer Denny looked solemnly into his note-book, though undoubtedly this was purely for show. "A Ms. Dawnya Rankin."

"Who's she?" whispered Carolyn to Holly; Holly shrugged.

"Are you going to take her into custody, or just question her here?" asked Tricia.

Officer Denny put on a very long face at this; he would have been a big success as the enter-tainment at a children's birthday party. I won-dered whether he was about to string her along and say that Ms. Dawnya Rankin would have to spend the night at the precinct house, but he merely said "I think we can handle her right here at the college."

"Gosh," said Tricia.

"What did she see?" demanded Holly.

Officer Denny looked mildly at us again. "That's what we aim to find out," he said. "Now if you fine, upstanding young people will permit, we'd like to go interview this Ms. Dawnya Rankin."

"I don't suppose we could come along ..." said Tricia wistfully.

The comparatively loquacious Officer Denny and the silent Officer Morales shook their heads and proceeded into that Hall which had previously occupied our attention: the Hall where lived Steve Madison, Liz MacKellar, Renee Gibeau, and Zoe Vogel. The Hall where, apparently, lived a new person for us to question: Ms. Dawnya Rankin.

14

"Rats," said Tricia for the **n**th time; "I really wanted to know what she saw. And now," she added, glancing at Pauline, "we're **really** late for class. D'you think George'll believe we got held up talking to the police?"

"I want to know about the blanket lint," said Holly. "You can't tell me there isn't something significant about a corpse being covered in blanket lint."

"Oh, it's probably from his own stupid blanket," said Carolyn. "He probably lay around on his bed all day doing nothing before he went off to get killed."

"Maybe," said Holly, looking most dissatisfied, "but I'll bet they're right and the murderer carried him over in a big old blanket. It'd certainly be the easiest way to carry him and avoid notice."

"This is true," I agreed, "but what of the lack of lint on the floor?"

"Well," said Holly, "it seems to me that a lot more lint would come off on his clothes than on the ground unless the blanket was positively **shedding**. I wish I'd thought to ask what kind of lint it was."

"I think his blanket ..." began Carolyn impetuously.

"I don't think it was **his** blanket," said Holly.

I pretended not to notice this little exchange; it seemed more prudent not to ask why Carolyn was familiar with the nature of Richard Gurney's blanket. True, I was eager to know the answer, but I had already noted the Gang of Four's disinclination to provide this sort of information. One of these days I was going to have to speak to Carolyn by herself, without three self-nominated censors leaping in to forestall me.

Now, however, we reluctantly agreed to go to class and wait till evening to tackle Ms. Dawnya Rankin. This was difficult; for despite the intrinsic interest of Voltaire and the Enlightenment, I found my attention wandering from our discussion of the red sheep in **Candide,** thus allowing one of the less inspired of my fellow students to get away with some unusually obtuse remarks. Instead of attending to the topic at hand and applying myself in a suitably scholarly fashion, or even gazing longingly out the window at the green grass and fine weather that awaited me, I was wondering what Dawnya Rankin had seen and why she had not mentioned it to the police until now. Had it been something obvious and terrifying, like seeing the murderer disposing of the body, or had it been something subtle whose importance she had only just realized? Not being familiar with Dawnya Rankin, I was at a loss to imagine what she might have noticed.

All of this being the case, I was relieved when class was over and I need no longer make a pretense of participation. Upon returning to the dorm, I located Dawnya's door, a relatively dull thing with little rainbows and bears on it indicating that Dawnya Rankin and Nila Ross lived there; but neither Dawnya nor Nila answered my knock, so I wandered down to the College Office again to see what Kathy and Linda were up to.

As usual, they seemed eager to cast down their filing and photocopying in favor of a chat.

"Look who's returned to the scene of the crime," said Linda as I entered their cubbyhole.

"Quick, call the cops, the real murderer's arrived," added Kathy. "Oh well, have you got any late-breaking gossip for us? Any more miniature funerals for illegal pets?"

Animals are not allowed in the dorms, though obviously this rule is frequently ignored.

"I thought of you the other day," said Linda. "Where did I put that thing?" She dug amid a pile of papers, surfacing triumphantly with one of startling azure. "Listen, we just got this in the mail: 'Noted author and mystic Heather Rosenbaum will speak—' ya-dee-ya-dee-ya ... 'As a child, Ms. Rosenbaum led funerals for neighborhood pets who had died.' Get that, Keith?"

"There's more," said Kathy, "like 'In high school she was introduced to the Tarot and Jungian psychology ...' but we'll spare you all of her Aquarian this-and-thats and transpersonal whosits."

"I like the part about the funerals being for pets 'who had died,'" I said. "I think it shows great delicacy of feeling that she refrained from holding funerals for pets who were still alive."

"True," said Linda. "Imagine coming home from work to find that the precocious little brat was out in back burying your darling Fluffy or your four-hundred-dollar parrot alive."

"Did you lead funerals as a child, Keith?" inquired Kathy sweetly.

I ignored this. "You'll be glad to know that we've had no more interments on our Hall, so unless Liz MacKellar's rabbit kicks the bucket ..."

"Liz MacKellar's rabbit'll kick a lot before he kicks the bucket," said Linda. "Isn't he the spotted one that peed on her boyfriend a few months ago?"

"Yes!" exclaimed Kathy. "That was a sight! Boyfriend was out in the Quad taking the mutt for a walk and it peed on his shoe—sprayed him in fact—so Boyfriend promptly whipped out his thing and responded in kind."

"Is Liz still enamored of this young man?" I inquired.

"Don't know," said Linda. "She approved at the time."

"Thought the rabbit got what he deserved," agreed Kathy. "Apparently he's jealous of the boyfriend. I hope Liz doesn't leave her room smelling like litterbox at the end of the year, or Theo'll have to slap some kind of damages on her."

"I understood that Hemingway prefers to mark her pillow," I said.

"Hemingway!" cried Kathy. **"Hemingway?"**

"Yes, she calls the rabbit Hemingway."

"That's beautiful," she went on. "I'll have to tell the other witnesses that the rabbit's name is Hemingway. It was one of those strange and interesting moments in the history of the Quad."

"Speaking of strange and interesting moments," I said, "there were some police here after lunch to speak with someone named Dawnya Rankin."

"Jeez, Keith, you don't miss a thing," said Linda. "How'd you know that?"

"We encountered them on the stairs on the way to class, of course."

Kathy threw up her hands. "We told 'em to wait till after class began so they wouldn't unnerve the populace so much. Didn't they wait?"

"Well, we were rather late to begin with," I pointed out, "and after talking to the police we were considerably later."

"What'd they want to talk to you for," said Kathy, "had you found a clue?"

"They were friendly enough," I said. "We wanted to know if they had made any progress, and they mentioned Dawnya Rankin."

"And?" said Linda.

"They said they had found lint on the corpse, suggesting he was carried in a blanket."

"Oh, whoop-de-do," said Kathy.

"Well," I said, "I want to know who Dawnya Rankin is and what she saw."

"So join the club," said Linda. "Come on, you talked to the police, didn't you worm it all out of them with your famous interrogation techniques?"

"You're staff," I said. "Didn't they tell you all about it?"

"What, the police unburden the secrets of their bosoms to a pair of lowly college secretaries?" said Kathy.

"Dream on," said Linda.

"Don't you even know who Dawnya Rankin is?" I persisted.

"Should I?" said Kathy.

"Is she the leader of a satanic cult?" said Linda. "I've never heard of her. Isn't she just some little frosh who has yet to make her mark on the world?"

"That's what I'm asking you," I said. "She wasn't in her room when I dropped by a few minutes ago, so all I know is that she had information for the police and that she has rainbows and bears on her door."

"Rainbows and bears?" said Kathy. "Definitely a frosh. Or a transfer from a junior college. Take her away."

"You're no use," I lamented.

"**Us!**" said Linda. "**You're** no use. You live in the dorms, you discovered the body, and all we can get out of you is that you don't know any more about Dawnya Rankin than we do, much less know what she spotted. At this rate all we can do is go back to work like the wage slaves we are."

"Wage slaves?" said another voice.

"Oh, hi Ferdinand," said both Kathy and Linda with just the merest soupçon of anxiety. "Keith won't surrender any more info about the murder, so we're stuck having to go back to our filing."

"Ah, Keith," said Ferdinand, turning to look at me for the first time. He pretended to examine me, as if I were a renowned but slippery character arriving from out of town, rather than a student he has known for several years. "Keith discovered the body, am I right?"

"Yes, Ferdinand," I said in that patient manner which so reveals one's true impatience.

"Must've been a shock, eh?"

"Somewhat," I agreed.

"Somewhat!" echoed Linda and Kathy disdainfully.

"It's very sad that such a thing should take place in this college," said Ferdinand.

I suppressed a yawn and tried to remember some of the piercing questions I had been meaning to ask him. After a moment I said "Why did it take so long for you to announce his death to the college?"

Ferdinand looked at me again, a trifle sharply, I thought. "Long? As a rule the university doesn't announce deaths at all. The only reason this one was announced was that it was felt that public safety might be involved. Even so, there was considerable discussion before it was decided to announce anything."

"Lovely," I said. "Are you saying that the university has a policy of hushing up death?"

For a second Ferdinand appeared irritated, but then his administrative air reasserted itself. "Keith, I'm afraid you don't quite understand, and that is natural enough." His hand strayed to his collar as if to adjust the tie that wasn't there. "The university does not 'hush up' death; it merely avoids publicizing it. When, as occasionally happens, a careless student drowns as a result of unsupervised swimming, or when another student fails to seek the aid of our counseling staff and instead seeks to end a period of depression by leaping from the top of a building, we do not 'hush up' their deaths; we first inform their families, and afterwards we have no objection if their friends wish to hold a quiet memorial service on campus.

We do not 'hush up' their deaths at all; but we do not believe that anything is gained by making announcements."

I remained unconvinced. "It still took a hell of a long time for you to announce a **murder,**" I said.

Ferdinand sighed. "I'm afraid you underestimate the difficulty of certain administrative decisions." Again, he seemed to regret not having a tie to straighten, though I had only rarely seen him wear one. "This was not my decision alone to make."

I was tempted to ask if he had been obliged to ask permission of the Board of Regents and the governor, but no doubt that would have been counterproductive of me.

Ferdinand smiled faintly. "Being provost of this college is not as easy a task as you might think."

"I suppose not, if you can't make your own decisions."

In the background, Kathy and Linda looked up with scandalized glee, then returned to their pretense of work.

"Keith, that is a rather extreme statement, and not what I meant to imply."

"Well ..." Ferdinand-baiting is always amusing, but this time I had to avoid antagonizing him, as there was no use in his simply turning his back and walking away.

"There is a considerable difference between a student dead by accident or his own hand, and a staff member who has obviously been murdered," said Ferdinand. "In the interest of public safety, it was deemed necessary to announce Richard's death to the college. However, it was not felt that the danger to the college was very great, and so far this has proved correct. It was felt that the police should be permitted time to investigate and perhaps clear up the matter immediately, and it was also felt that the announcement should be postponed until most of the student body was in residence—which, as you know, is not the case on weekends."

I was finding Ferdinand's officialese more and more repugnant, with his "it was also felts," which sounded to me like fundamental avoidance of action. Even though I was not wandering around in fear, I saw little to support his optimism about our safety.

"What's the university's policy on rape and assault?" I asked.

"Keith, let's not worry about these things just now," said Ferdinand. "You've been through a very unpleasant experience, and I sympathize with your concern, but—"

"Let me just ask you something else, then," I said. "What did you think of Richard Gurney, personally?"

15

"Ferdinand is such a dolt sometimes!" exclaimed Holly when I described my encounter with the Provost at dinner. "I mean, **really**."

We were sitting, as usual, in the noise and squalor of the dining room; around us forks were digging into the college's uninspired version of sweet and sour pork, while vegetarians contended with a form of sweet and sour without pork. Holly and Carolyn's reaction to my tale of Ferdinand was distinctly sour.

"'The university does not "hush up" death!'" repeated Carolyn irritably. "What a line. What's he going to do now, hold a press conference?"

"Ferdinand is so obsessed with being an administrator," said Holly. "It's no wonder he only finds time to teach one class. He's too busy pontificating about how important his duties are, and how he can't make unilateral decisions. It's no wonder his wife spends all her time making ugly pottery; she probably can't stand listening to him."

"Considering that he doesn't seem to care whether we kill ourselves or get killed by wandering bears ..." said Carolyn. She shut her eyes and, by some odd process of association, recited:

> The common cormorant or shag
> Lays eggs inside a paper bag
> But what these unobservant birds
> Have never noticed is that herds
> Of wandering bears may come with buns
> And steal the bags to hold the crumbs.

"What?" said Holly. "What's that from?"

"Oh, I don't know," said Carolyn, opening her eyes.

"What do bears have to do with anything?"

"Nothing."

"Well," said Holly, with her usual refusal to stray from the facts or her version of them, "I'm very surprised that Ferdinand would admit to not worrying whether the rest of us were about to get killed."

"That wasn't exactly what he said."

"Of course not, but that's what he meant. How does he know that one of us doesn't have some kind of valuable information that the murderer is about to kill for, or kill to hide? Really, Ferdinand is a complete idiot."

"Do you mean one of **us,** or students in general?" I inquired.

"Either," said Holly carelessly. "For all we know, **we** know something the murderer would kill for. Then again, I bet a lot of people do."

"Like what?" said Carolyn.

"Who knows?" said Holly.

I put down my fork. "I suppose it all comes down to why Richard Gurney was murdered."

"If we knew that ..." said Carolyn, twisting her bracelet absent-mindedly. "We don't even know if it was premeditated."

"Don't be silly," said Holly, "it must've been premeditated. People don't just haul off and kill people on the spur of the moment."

"They do too," said Carolyn.

"They do it all the time," I said.

"You know what I mean," said Holly, "if it's unpremeditated, people kill each other in fights. They don't walk up to each other in dorm Halls and knock each other off, like characters in a western or something."

"Well, how do we know he wasn't killed in a fight?" said Carolyn.

"He didn't look like he'd been in a fight, did he? Nobody gets into that kind of a fight in a dorm, anyway."

"It wouldn't have to have been a fist fight," I remarked. "Fist fights start out as arguments. Maybe this was the first blow."

"Quite a lethal first blow," said Malcolm, joining us. "They've put out the desserts," he added.

"Oh, leather brownies again," said Carolyn, prodding the one on his plate.

"People get carried away," I said. "They say things they regret, they hit people too hard—"

"Maybe," said Holly, "but ten to one the murderer planned this job ahead. I'll bet Gurney knew something the murderer didn't want to get out, or did something the murderer didn't like, or something like that."

"Maybe Gurney was a blackmailer," suggested Malcolm between mouthfuls. "Classically speaking, blackmailers are always good candidates for murder."

"Classically speaking, yes," I agreed, "but this is not 1890 or 1910. Blackmail no longer has the appeal it once did. Haven't we already discounted this out of sheer improbability?"

"No," said Holly.

"Ferdinand did it," said Carolyn. "The perfect solution. At least, it's the perfect solution if you keep rejecting the idea that someone killed Gurney in revulsion at his stupid advances."

"Why Ferdinand?" inquired Malcolm. "Is there news on the Ferdinand front?"

There were exclamations from Holly and Carolyn at our idiocy in having failed to tell Malcolm of my encounter with the Provost. After briefly excusing myself to go and pour another glass of milk, I repeated my tale for his benefit.

"It's all very interesting," he said when I paused, "though none of it strikes me as at all out of character for Ferdinand or any other administrator. But what did he say when you asked what he thought of Gurney personally?"

I returned mentally to the College Office, where Kathy and Linda had pretended to Xerox and file while Ferdinand and I stood on the rather dingy green industrial carpeting next to the boxes of add- and drop-class forms, fencing questions and pompous nothings back and forth. Despite the open door, it had seemed hot and stuffy in the office, and Ferdinand's insistence on straightening and re-straightening the tie that wasn't there had made me feel both overheated and impatient. As he spoke, I had found myself entertaining the distracting and useless hope that upon my eventual graduation I would **not** be obliged to wear a tie to work. But I had listened to his tedious and self-serving mouthings, and finally I had demanded his opinion of Richard Gurney. I had not expected much from this question, and perhaps I had not gotten much either. Or had I and not known it? I had asked, and Ferdinand had looked away out the window to some unspecified sector of Damson House. I had not been able to see whether his expression was one of boredom, anxiety, distrust, or impatience as he gazed out the window and said:

"Now honestly, Keith, what is the point in asking me a question like that? Richard is dead, and I have no reason anymore to have any opinion at all about him. It is not as though he was a friend of mine, or as though we worked closely together." Then Ferdinand had turned back to face me. With a trace of a smile, he said "He was only here for a few months, maybe a year. I didn't get to know him the way I have some of our more pesky students like you. Now don't you have a class to go to, or some studying to do?"

Thus dismissed, I had spent the remainder of the afternoon alternately reading and staring out my window at the College Office, making ill-conceived doodles with a leaky technical pen. Neither Voltaire and the Enlightenment, nor the ins and outs of European Diplomatic History, had seemed able to hold my attention.

"That was probably unusually candid of Ferdinand," commented Malcolm.

"Why do you say that?" I asked.

"Well, I would have expected him to be a little smoother about it, to give you some of that nonsense about not speaking ill of the dead, or about how sad the whole business is."

"Hmm," I said. "Implying dislike without actually saying so?"

"Maybe not dislike," admitted Malcolm; "it sounds like he was still pretty cagey. But definitely trying to distance himself. After all, isn't it a little odd when a man not only claims to have hardly known a subordinate, but insists that the other man's being dead renders his own opinion moot?"

"Suppose that Ferdinand **did** do it," said Holly, "and suppose that he did it because Gurney was blackmailing him." She whipped out her ever-present appointment book and pencil, without which one suspects her life would come to a very ruffled halt, and turned to the back of a used page. "What would Gurney have been blackmailing him about?"

"First," I interjected, "who was Gurney threatening to spill to? I mean, let's be thorough about this."

"I am," said Holly. "I'm putting it all in **outline**."

"How disgusting," murmured Carolyn, leaning over Holly's diagram. Presumably she referred to Holly's command of the outline method and its formality, as Holly had not yet marked beyond a Roman numeral or two.

"As far as I know, one could either blackmail Ferdinand by threatening to tell his wife, or by threatening to tell the university," I said. "I can easily imagine Ferdinand indulging in activities that he wouldn't want Claudia to know about, but I doubt he'd care enough to pay blackmail."

"Does he have access to college funds?" inquired Carolyn. "Maybe he was dipping into them ..."

Holly scribbled in her book. "Wouldn't the Bursar be in charge of the money?" she said. "Not that that would stop a real embezzler."

"Damn," I said. "I hadn't thought of the Bursar. Another person to suspect! Oh well, let's keep to Ferdinand for the moment." I didn't care to admit that I had forgotten the Bursar's name; she had never given me cause to remember it, though I had often seen it affixed to the helpful little pamphlets the college distributes each year advising us how to live in the dorms.

"Presumably Ferdinand's crime would either be financial or one of moral turpitude," said Malcolm. "I don't think we're likely to discover that his Ph.D. is a fraud."

"I have an idea," said Carolyn suddenly. "What if the blackmail weren't a question of something Ferdinand had already done, but something Gurney was trying to get him to do?"

"That doesn't make sense," said Holly.

"Well, I mean that Gurney wanted to get Ferdinand to do something that Ferdinand didn't want to do ..."

"What on earth would he want Ferdinand to do?" said Holly.

"Who knows?" said Carolyn. "We're only inventing scenarios; it's not as though we're convinced Ferdinand whacked him and we just can't think why."

"Yes, but how could he leverage Ferdinand if Ferdinand hadn't already done something?"

"Hell if I know."

"Well, it's an interesting concept," said Malcolm, "but it doesn't alter the fundamental assumption of blackmail."

"It gives us yet another permutation to wonder about," I said, "which may be good or may be bad. We can sit around till doomsday imagining different possibilities—and naturally we must—but who knows whether any of them will be right."

"Or, even if they're right," said Carolyn, "whether they have anything to do with the murder."

"Ah yes," said Malcolm, "the swarm of innocent suspects, each with something different to hide. Very neat, very true to form. Locate everyone who has a guilty secret, and you'll still only have one murderer." He grinned wryly and stood up. "See you all later ... I've got to go talk to JoAnne."

We watched his slim, wiry, bicyclist's form drop off his tray on the conveyor belt and ascend the stairs to the lobby. Then, suddenly, Holly exclaimed "Shit! We forgot to tell him the most exciting news of all!"

We had forgotten to tell him about Dawnya Rankin.

16

Once back at the Hall, Holly, Carolyn and I became embroiled in a discussion of how to approach the unknown Dawnya Rankin. I favored the simple approach, in which one or another of us would knock on her door, introduce ourselves as among the discoverers of the body, and say that we had heard she too had seen or heard something. Holly, on the other hand, scorned this idea and asserted that we must come up with some manner of ingenious ploy, while Carolyn professed interest in both schemes but declined the role of interlocutor. It struck me that, for a reasonably outgoing person, Carolyn was unusually reluctant to speak to anyone she did not already know, and I wondered whether she was normally this diffident or whether this was only true in matters concerning Richard Gurney. I realized that, as a friend and hallmate of Carolyn's, I had never actually had cause to observe how she behaved when confronted with new people; there had been nothing to note about anyone she had ever met in my presence, and I had never found her shy in a purely social context.

Still, it was true that Carolyn had more of a quiet side than the rest of the Gang of Four—despite the fact that she could equal any of them for noise when in the mood—and she had less of an interest in college politics and scandals than did Holly, Evan, or I. So although I might wonder whether her avoidance of the interrogator's role was a result of some tie to Richard Gurney, I could not assume this to be the case.

In the midst of our discussion, we were interrupted by the advent of JoAnne, our R.A.

"Hey, guys, what's up?" said JoAnne as she approached, flyers and staple-gun in hand.

"Oh, life as usual, I guess," said Carolyn mendaciously.

"I hear you discovered the body," went on JoAnne, leaning companionably against the wall. "Malcolm was telling me about it. I don't know whether to wish I'd been there or be glad I wasn't."

"As bodies go, it was probably rather tame," I said, "but we found it exciting enough."

"At least he hadn't started to stink yet," said Carolyn. Holly made a face.

"I wonder what the usual psychological reaction is to coming across dead people?" mused JoAnne.

"Well, what would you have done?"

"Oh, hard to say. I'm just wondering if I ought to study your responses in case I ever need a good topic for a paper."

Holly compressed her lips in a censorious way; she does not have a high opinion of JoAnne, and feels that she herself would be well-suited to the position of R.A.

"But anyway," said JoAnne, "the reason I came down is that I thought it'd be fun to have a movie night tomorrow. Malcolm's arranging to get the movies and a projector, and I'll make popcorn. Can you all be there?"

We agreed that we probably could, and demanded to know the program.

"I'm not sure yet," said JoAnne. "It depends a little on what he can get. We were thinking it'd be fun to get a lot of old silents, but the film classes might have those checked out. Anyway, it'll be a blast."

She resumed stuffing flyers under doors and stapled what sounded like several to the board in the bathroom, then vanished with a wave and a cheery "See you!"

"That sounds like fun," said Carolyn.

"We should've asked her what she thought about Richard Gurney," said Holly.

"JoAnne is easy to find," I said. "We won't have any trouble asking her—for all we know, Malcolm already has."

"**Maybe,**" said Holly darkly. "I think she's making a play for him."

Carolyn and I burst out laughing at this. It was not that we could not imagine JoAnne attracted to Malcolm, with his pleasant features, mild manner, and fondness for study; it was that Holly should display such absurd jealousy in a matter that did not concern her in the least.

"Don't be silly," said Carolyn. "JoAnne's not after Malcolm. Anyway, what about Dawnya Rankin?"

Footsteps sounded from the other end of the Hall. "Who's Dawnya Rankin?" inquired Evan.

There was a slight pause; neither Holly nor Carolyn appeared eager to vouchsafe him information.

"Dawnya Rankin," I said, "is a woman who may hold a clue to the death of Richard Gurney."

Evan joined us in leaning against the wall, though as usual his posture remained so erect that one hesitated to put his stance in the same class as the easy slouches practiced by the rest of us. "A clue?" he said. "What sort of clue?"

"We have no idea," said Holly. "According to the police, she noticed something suspicious."

"Consequently," said Carolyn, "we want to find out **what.**"

"Well, what's stopping you?" said Evan. "Why don't you ask her? Or have the police taken her into custody?"

"We have been trying to determine," I said, "the best method for approaching her."

Evan looked disgusted at our slow progress, and indicated that he would go ask Dawnya right away, if we would but divulge her whereabouts.

"Evan Reid!" said Holly. "You can't just barge in on someone like that."

"Why not?"

"Because you just can't."

Evan stared at her. "I fail to see the difference between my asking Dawnya Rankin a question, and you and Malcolm interrogating Steve Madison."

Holly sank back slightly against the wall, unwilling or unable to refute this.

"The only decision to be made," said Evan, "and I am perfectly ready to make it myself, is who should speak to the woman."

"I'll talk to her," said Holly.

"Yes, but you'll spend forever thinking up a plan," I said.

"There's no need for any cockamamie **plan,**" said Evan. "We simply go and knock on her door."

"Well, let's get it over with," said Carolyn. "Why don't the two of you go together, or all of us can go and hint that there's a SWAT team waiting outside."

Simultaneously perceiving the uselessness of this discussion, the four of us went into the next Hall and towards Dawnya's bear-and-rainbowed door, only to be met by Tricia and Liz emerging, rabbit at heel, from Liz's room.

"It's no use," said Tricia. "Dawnya's gone."

"Gone?" we repeated. "How gone?"

"She's gone to the Health Center," explained Liz. "She was too upset to stay in her room."

"Too upset?" said Holly. "What happened? Are you sure she's really at the Health Center?"

"Well, I didn't follow her there," said Liz, bending to scoop up Hemingway, who then sat looking over her shoulder with ears in the air and an expression of fierce interest. "But she's supposed to be spending the night there calming down."

"But why now?" I said. We were all puzzled that she would be upset now rather than whenever she noticed whatever she had noticed. Unless ...

"What if she had just noticed something in the last day or two?" said Carolyn.

"The murderer disposing of the blanket, or something," said Holly.

Liz glanced uneasily up and down the hall. "Why don't you all come in, if we're going to talk about murderers. Who knows who might be listening?"

We assented, and crowded into her surprisingly spotless abode. For a woman with an incontinent rabbit, she succeeded in maintaining a remarkably white and virginal atmosphere, which would not have been out of place in the bedroom of a debutante. At the head of the white quilted bedspread, there sat a cluster of white cutwork and lace pillows cushioning the back of a very new plush stuffed bear. The wardrobe unit displayed a series of bouffant gowns replete with taffeta and netting, and two bottles of perfume could be seen on the dresser in front of the mirror in the company of an elegant comb and hairbrush set. What with all of these Young Miss accoutrements, I was relieved to see Hemingway's cage atop a bed of newspaper in the corner, and a pile of books by Dostoyevsky, the Brontës, and other nineteenth-century novelists spilling across the windowsill.

We settled ourselves gingerly on the immaculate bed and the surrounding environs, and Liz said "Maybe I'm being paranoid, but after all, nobody knows who killed him. It might even have been somebody on my Hall."

"Do you know your Hall very well?" asked Evan.

"Some people," said Liz, "some people not. It's not like your Hall—people just kind of do their thing and maybe you get to know them and maybe you don't."

"Did you know Dawnya Rankin very well?" asked Holly.

"Oh, a little," said Liz.

"You make it sound like she's dead," protested Carolyn in a whisper.

"For all I know, she is," returned Holly.

"What is she like?" said Evan, ignoring the possibility that Dawnya had not survived her interview with Officers Denny and Morales.

Liz shrugged. "Sort of quiet, I guess. I never paid much attention to her. She's an Econ major or something boring like that."

Evan frowned, and I recalled that he had given brief consideration to the Econ major some months earlier. At the time he had felt that only the study of economic theory could assist him in his ongoing search for meaning, but Econ had proved a mere passing fancy. It had soon yielded to Chinese and the Tao.

"I can't tell you a whole lot about her," Liz went on. "By dinnertime, people knew that the police had come by and that she went to the Health Center after that. I think our RA went over with her. But we didn't know much more than that. Like I said, this Hall is pretty dull. Nobody pays much attention to anyone else."

"Do you think it's very likely that the murderer might live on your Hall?" asked Tricia excitedly, petting Hemingway with a vigor he seemed to enjoy.

"No, of course not," said Liz; "you just never know. I mean, when somebody shows up dead practically next door …"

"Yes," said Carolyn.

"Well," I said, "who exactly does live on your Hall? We've been racking our brains and come up with nothing, and now this Dawnya Rankin, whom none of us had even heard of, has come up with something and been interviewed by the police." After all, if we had merely wanted a list of names, we could have walked through the Hall and written them down off people's doors, but Liz was an insider and I felt she ought to know something about her neighbors, even if it was only a matter of vague impressions.

Liz thought for a moment. "There's Dawnya and her roommate Nila, of course," she said.

"Wait," said Holly, throwing open her appointment book to the unused back of yet another page.

"What's Nila like?" said Tricia. "D'you think Dawnya saw Nila do something and now she's in the Health Center for her own protection?"

"Oh, I don't think it was Nila," said Liz. "I'm sure Nila didn't know or care that Richard Gurney existed."

"That's true of most people," muttered Carolyn.

"Well, who else is there?"

"Jerry and Doug ..." said Liz. "I don't know much about them, except they're both kind of cute and Jerry plays guitar."

"What about Steve Madison?" I asked.

"Oh, he lives out by the trash chute," said Liz. "I hardly ever see him. I mean, he's friendly enough, but ..."

"He claims he didn't notice anything unusual the night of the murder," said Evan. "Do you think that's likely?"

"Oh, absolutely," said Liz. "He spends most of his time playing his stereo and smoking doobies. Well, maybe not smoking doobies all the time; he's not a total stoner or anything. Not like Lainey Silver or Gilbert or those people who decorate their doors with pinups of pot plants from **High Times**."

"Lainey isn't on your Hall, is she?" said Tricia.

Liz laughed. "No way! My RA can't stand her. She's on the next Hall, but out by the stairs like Steve Madison."

"Well, who else is on your Hall?" I asked. "You've got Renee Gibeau and Zoe Vogel—"

"**They** certainly didn't do it," said Liz. "Gee, can you imagine Renee or Zoe killing someone?"

"Renee wouldn't kill anybody," said Tricia.

"Obviously," said Liz. "Or Zoe either. Besides, Zoe's never around. She probably didn't even know Richard Gurney."

"Yes she did," said Tricia. "Remember, you told us that he came on to her at that sherry party?"

"Oh, right," said Liz. "Well, she still wouldn't have killed him."

"It is hard to see how she could have," said Evan, "when she is so small."

We all sighed. The strength required to lift Richard Gurney seemed a great stumbling block no matter whose name we mentioned. Still, there was a name we had not mentioned for some time, and it was attached to a person who could probably—albeit with some difficulty—have lifted Gurney.

"Have you ever noticed Ferdinand wandering around your Hall?" I inquired.

17

"Ferdinand!" said Liz, "d'you mean the Provost?"

"What other Ferdinand do we know?"

"Well, shoot, I don't know. Why would the Provost visit our Hall?"

"He sure doesn't visit **ours**," said Carolyn from the floor, where she and Tricia were now burying their faces in the recumbent Hemingway's fur and Tricia was making occasional murmurs and yelps of "Hemmy-poo! What a fat bun-bun you are!"

I ignored these outbreaks of babytalk and said "It had occurred to us that Ferdinand might be involved in the murder."

Liz leaned back on her spotless bed. "Why Ferdinand?" she said.

"Because he avoided announcing the murder until Tuesday. Because he was very evasive when I talked to him this afternoon."

"Ferdinand's always evasive," said Evan. "He's an administrator. Do you mean he was more evasive than usual?"

"That's hard to say. But I think he makes a better suspect than the average student, at least if we credit Malcolm's hypothesis that Gurney was blackmailing someone. What could Gurney blackmail a student about?"

"Not very much," conceded Holly.

There was a pause. Then Evan said "I have no objection to suspecting Ferdinand, but we have no basis for supposing Richard Gurney was blackmailing him."

"Evan," I said, "in a situation where motive is so nebulous, and suspects are either few or countless depending on your point of view, we must proceed with one or more hypotheses, and either prove or disprove them. Ferdinand may not be the murderer, but if he isn't, we may be able to prove it. In the meantime, we can still suspect the entire population of this college."

"This is enough to make anyone's head swim," said Liz. "You can't suspect an entire college—that's at least four hundred people!"

"Holland House is temporarily out of the picture," said Evan. "But I agree that it's best to concentrate on Ferdinand and a few other geographically likely souls."

"Geographically likely!" said Carolyn. "Geographically in terms of where he lived, or where he was killed?"

Gurney had lived in a dark little suite on the ground floor, probably the least desirable of all the preceptor apartments. It had two or three small windows, high for privacy, that looked out upon a concrete retaining wall and were shaded by the enormous pines protected by that wall. Being a studio arrangement, it boasted essentially only one room plus a bathroom cubicle, as the kitchen was but an extension of the rest. I had not been inside since Gurney's arrival, but his predecessor, Lynette Holmes, had called it a hole in the wall and an ugly cave. There were not many students sharing the ground floor with him, and their equally dark rooms were not close to his. Geographically speaking, I did not think his place of residence was nearly as significant as his place of death—wherever that was.

"Well, if we knew where he was killed ..." said Tricia.

"All the evidence points to this Hall," said Evan.

"This very Hall," said Holly, and Liz looked glum.

"He wasn't killed on **our** Hall," I said, "because we were there."

"The only way he couldn't've been killed on your Hall was if he was killed on the stairs, or in the elevator, or next to the trash," said Carolyn.

"If you haven't seen Ferdinand roaming around," I said, "or any other staff who have no business here, then for the moment we had better concentrate on your hallmates."

It was a dreary consultation, and after it was done we did not feel as though we had gotten much farther than when we had started. Besides Steve Madison, Dawnya and Nila, Zoe and Renee, Jerry and Doug, and Pam the RA, there was a bewildering but innocent-sounding list of "Wally and John, Panda and Ellen, Bruce and Brian, Karie and Janet, Jordan and Tom, Kurt and Terry," and so on. We could not glean anything of remarkable interest about any of these people, leaving us a disappointed if marginally more knowledgeable group. This was especially true since we felt cheated at not having been able to interview Dawnya Rankin; we felt sure that if only we could have spoken with Dawnya Rankin, we would have learned the answers to many questions.

However, we could only presume that Dawnya Rankin would emerge from the Health Center at some point during the following day, so with that in mind, we finally left Liz and Hemingway to their joint study of the Victorian novel.

"I don't suppose we can come up with anything more tonight," said Evan as we returned to our Hall; he aimed a few kicks at the wall and nearly achieved a hole in the plaster.

"It does seem as though we would be wise to study or sleep or something of that sort," I agreed.

At this point Tricia exclaimed "Bagels!"

"With Swiss cheese," added Carolyn, and with little more ado they and Holly were grabbing their wallets and vanishing in the direction of the coffee shop. Evan and I retired more sedately to our rooms.

The next morning it occurred to me that I had not asked Theo Roth anything about Ferdinand, nor about Ferdinand's attitude towards Richard Gurney, nor about any of the rest of the staff or RAs. It now seemed to me that my questioning of Theo had been woefully inadequate, and that I could surely improve upon my previous efforts.

Accordingly, around ten o'clock I ventured back to Holland House and Theo's office, noting as I did so the delightful warmth of the sun and the damp, verdant fragrance of the shrubs and grass in the Quad. Murder apart, spring seemed to promise well this year.

I found Theo in his office, hunched over some paperwork that, judging by the expression on his face, was of a peculiarly odious nature. When he looked up and saw me, he did not smile quite so happily as usual, though he gestured for me to sit down.

"If this is an inconvenient time, I can always come back later," I said.

"Nah, no problem," said Theo. "One time's just as inconvenient as another." He jabbed his pen at one of the papers. "Life is really a bitch sometimes."

I agreed politely, and asked what was on his mind this fine morning.

"Goddamn paperwork about that goddamn jerk Richard Gurney, pardon my French," said Theo. "I wish to God I'd never set eyes on him."

This was a propitious start if I had ever heard one. All I had to do was make a good follow-up.

"What kind of paperwork is it?" I inquired.

"Oh, every kind of shit you can possibly imagine," said Theo disgustedly. "I have to close out all my files on him, do the paperwork to get him off the payroll, look over his university insurance coverage, find out who gets his life insurance, wonder what the hell we're supposed to do with his stuff and whether we should hire someone to take his place yet. Basically, a lot of administrative bull that I never imagined in my worst nightmares."

"I would've thought the Bursar would be handling a lot of that," I said, remembering the possibility of the Bursar embezzling funds.

"Well, she will, but I have to do all the preliminary shitwork," said Theo. "I hired him, so I have to weed through everything and fill in the blanks and make everything look presentable and easy to read. Then I give it all to Jan and she does whatever she has to do and passes on whatever gets passed on. Bureaucracy! I guess I should be grateful that I don't have to send memos around in triplicate every time somebody sneezes." Theo scratched his head and sighed.

"Does the University have to notify his next of kin and beneficiaries, or does the insurance company do that?"

"Oh, we had to notify the next of kin," said Theo. "But I think the insurance company deals with the beneficiaries."

"Did you notice who they are?"

"The beneficiaries?" said Theo. "No, I haven't gotten to that one yet. Probably his family. Wait, let me see—now you've got me curious. After all, he was murdered."

Theo thumbed through the papers on his desk.

"Ah, here it is, life insurance benefits. Generous of the University to give us life insurance instead of more pay, huh? Give us the last thing most of us are likely to need?"

"The University still pays better than anyone else in town," I said, and it was true. The other two major employers in the area, a gum facto-ry and an amusement park, specialized in minimum-wage positions. In order to find better pay, the average citizen had to drive an hour or more every morning on a notoriously serpentine road.

"Well, I guess elderly professors want life insurance," said Theo. "And married people who go in for sky diving and hang gliding. I think I wrote in my mother on mine, or maybe my brother." He tapped the paper and sat back. "Anyway, it looks like Richard Gurney's beneficiary is somebody named Mary Fitchen."

"Mary Fitchen?" I said. "Who's she?"

"Damned if I know," said Theo. "But like I say, probably a relative. People don't usually name their friends as beneficiaries; friends change, or move around, or whatever." He examined the document again, saying "Still, it'd be interesting to know."

"I thought you had to notify the next of kin," I said.

"Well, we did," said Theo; "that is, we told the police who to notify."

"Well, was Mary Fitchen one of the next of kin?"

Theo gazed briefly at the ceiling and then back at me. "Hell if I know. People don't list the whole goddamn clan on their employment forms, they just put down one or two people to contact if they get run over by a bus."

"But Mary Fitchen wasn't one of those people?" I persisted. Really, Theo was being unusually dense, considering that as far as I knew he had nothing to hide.

"I don't think he listed anyone named Fitchen."

"Have you checked to see if she's a student?"

"No." Theo tugged at his sand-colored mustache and regarded me with interest. "Do I get the impression that you think Gurney was murdered for his life insurance?" he demanded.

I sat back in my chair and affected to check the progress of my morning stubble. It was the same as it was every morning: stubble. Some mornings it was one day long, some mornings two or three. On the whole, I am a little too pleased with the shape of my face to obscure it with excess facial hair, but Theo's beard and mustache were probably an improvement on his.

"No, I don't especially think Gurney was murdered for his insurance," I said, "but one must consider every angle."

"Am I correct," said Theo amiably, "in assuming that you've suddenly turned into a private eye?"

I undertook a more careful investigation of my stubble. After all, there was always the possibility that it was longer on one side than the other, which would mean that either I favored one side when shaving, or that the beard I did not plan to grow would have been lopsided. One does not want a lopsided beard, even if it is totally hypothetical.

"I was one of the people who found him," I said in injured tones.

Theo laughed. "Hey, you can poke around all you want for all I care," he said. "I didn't kill him! And I don't want murderers roaming the campus, either. Personally, I think that between you and Holly and the police, the killer doesn't stand a chance."

"What, has Holly been in asking questions too?"

"Oy, Jesus, has she ever!" Theo sat back in his chair again and I wondered why I hadn't heard about this before.

18

"Keith, that woman is like a bloodhound once she gets started," said Theo, "or a terrier. She just keeps **on**."

"When did you talk to her?" I asked.

"Oh, shit, I don't know ... maybe a few days ago. Is she always that hard to satisfy?"

"It depends," I said.

"Let me tell you, she can be tenacious! I wonder if she's like that with her boyfriend?"

I felt that this was beside the point. "He graduated," I said. "Maybe now she has to do something new to burn off all the excess calories that used to be his responsibility."

"I don't know whether it was a mistake or a damn good thing that I didn't hire her to be your RA. Probably a good thing, but you'd know better than me."

I avoided the topic of Holly-as-RA. "What all did she ask you?"

"Oh, I don't know exactly what," said Theo. "You should ask her, not me. Or aren't you speaking?"

"I thought we were," I replied.

"Well, ask me whatever you want, but don't ask me what Holly asked me, 'cause I don't remember."

I contemplated the curious logic, or illogic, of this sentence. Then I said "Actually, I'd like to know whatever you know about Gurney's social life. Who he spent time with, who disliked him, what kinds of things he did, what people had to say about him."

"That's a tall order," said Theo. He seemed to be deciding whether to amplify this, when the phone rang.

We both jumped at the unexpected interruption.

"'Scuse me," said Theo automatically, reaching for the receiver. "Hello—Housing, Theo speaking."

As he spoke, I amused myself with the thought that, from the looks of the beige plastic on the telephone, a fingerprint squad would have a field day should they ever attempt to explore its surface. Theo's handset and receiver, and even the spiral cord connecting the two, appeared to feature not just the normal complement of marks and smears, but a degree of layering suited to the talents of an archaeologist, a veritable palimpsest of prints. I was amazed that anyone could achieve this effect without the help of small and sticky children.

"Shit, Ferdinand," Theo was saying, "I'm doing everything I can already. Believe me, the paperwork will be in Jan's box as fast as I can get it there."

Ferdinand? Why was he calling? I abandoned my archaeological and anthropological speculations, and began to listen to the conversation.

"Okay," said Theo, "I hear you, Ferdinand. I get the picture." He sighed. "Right. Bye."

He returned the receiver to its cradle without excessive delicacy, and I said "I had been meaning to ask you about Ferdinand's role in all of this."

Theo seemed scarcely to notice my question, exclaiming "Ferdinand! Don't talk to me about Ferdinand!" Then he appeared to remember my existence, and said "Look, I can't talk anymore, I've got to get these papers finished and turned in to Jan before somebody barbecues me."

"Why was Ferdinand calling you himself?" I asked. "Can't the Bursar make her own phone calls?"

"I don't know," said Theo, looking harassed. "They want this stuff yesterday, so I can't sit around bullshitting with you anymore. Sorry."

"That's okay," I said, though in truth I was quite disappointed, even if not actually prostrate with grief. I arose and left him to his work, wondering who Mary Fitchen was and why Ferdinand had suddenly felt the need to prod Theo back into motion. Had he chanced to see us through the large office window, or had some higher authority demanded that the matter be wrapped up, or ...?

I glanced at my watch, and realized that in any case it was almost time for me to get to class. I had not prepared much to say about the week's reading, and there were only five other students in the seminar, so this might prove to be a bit of a problem. Still, I felt that one did not often have the opportunity to investigate murders, and that some concessions could be made in this regard. My guilt temporarily banished, I went to my room and retrieved my notebooks.

However, after a less than satisfactory showing in class and a late and even more unsatisfactory lunch, I deemed it best to retreat into study, even if only for a while. Accordingly, I decamped to the library, where, after returning various completed or useless or overdue books, I sought out some journal articles that had been recommended to me, and settled myself with these in one of the large square stuffed-vinyl chairs that surround the racks of periodicals.

The chair was comfortable and the air for once only slightly warmer than that outside (generally it is a minimum of ten degrees hotter, enabling library employees to work in a state of near undress), and for an hour or so I read attentively, or at least diligently, about the ways and achievements of such diverse diplomatic figures as Talleyrand, Woodrow Wilson, Neville Chamberlain, Edvard Beneš, and Otto von Bismarck. As the articles dealt with a variety of periods and countries, before long I found myself speculating how the boundaries of Europe might have changed had Beneš had Talleyrand's assistance in creating Czechoslovakia, or had Chamberlain attempted to appease Napoleon rather than Hitler. Or what if Germany or Italy had unified earlier, or if Poland had not been divided, or if the Rhineland had succeeded as an independent state.

Realizing that this sort of thing was unlikely to advance my understanding of the actual events, I lifted my head to clear my thoughts, and noticed Zoe Vogel leafing through a pamphlet at a nearby rack.

"Hey, Zoe," I said, "what would Europe be like today if Austro-Hungary and the Ottoman Empire were still in existence?"

She started upon hearing her name, then turned and saw me. Her face seemed paler than usual, and I wondered if the flu she had claimed to worry about and that Renee had denied knowledge of was in fact some other, less mundane sickness. On the other hand, if her relationship with Lina Troyer was a serious one—and I knew no reason to believe it was not—she was probably under considerable stress.

She smiled and said "What if Hitler had been content to paint little postcards, or if Franco had been defeated in '37?"

"What if the British had never colonized India?"

She put the pamphlet down. "What if Belgium had stayed out of the Congo? Joseph Conrad would never have written **Heart of Darkness.**" Having said that, her smile faded slightly.

"Well, we can also imagine a historical situation in which he would never have left Poland," I said.

She grinned and came and sat down on the wooden table that linked my chair to the next. "What're you doing, inventing a history game?"

"No, just frittering away my study time," I admitted. "What with finding dead bodies strewn hither and yon, my powers of concentration aren't what they used to be."

There was a slight pause. Then she said "What do you mean, dead bodie_s_—wasn't there only one?"

"Well, yes," I said, "so far ... but finding him was quite enough. Besides, once one dead body shows up, more are sure to follow."

"I didn't know you found him," said Zoe.

"Well, technically I suppose Holly did, but the rest of us were right behind."

"Why? Where was he?" Even her voice sounded pale. Clearly I was going to have to ask her about this Lina Troyer business, and if possible come up with something helpful, though I could not imagine what.

"We found him in the trash," I said lightly. "He was sitting on the recyclable-glass can. I can tell you, it was a distinct surprise; we were only trying to dispose of Carolyn's dead hamster."

"How strange," said Zoe, but she did not really seem to be listening. "I guess I missed out on hearing all these things; I'm never in the dorm anymore." She thought for a moment. "I spent the whole weekend at Bronwen's."

I resisted the impulse to pat her hand; she had never been averse to ordinary friendly gestures of that sort, but somehow I was not sure she would welcome them just now. Instead, I said "I would've thought you'd be over at Lina Troyer's."

"I had my reasons!" said Zoe, and then, "Why does everybody have to know all of my business?"

As this did not seem so much a personal attack as a complaint against the world, I said "People usually notice that sort of thing."

"You mean relationships between students and faculty."

"Were you trying to keep it a secret?"

"Well, I hadn't really thought about it until Lina's tenure came up. Mostly I just thought about the same things you think about in any relationship. I mean, it's not like I was ashamed of it, or like I was being victimized. Lina's just ..." Her voice caught, but she recovered. "I just happen to love her."

Zoe was silent for some time, and I did not press her.

"She's such a wonderful person, and I just want to be with her, and look at her, and talk, and all those other things. I wish she already had her tenure, but how could she? She was only twenty-seven when she got her Ph.D." Zoe paused again. "The whole thing is just fucked," she said. "They don't want her because she's gay, but they can't argue about her ability, or her publication record, or whatever else ..."

"There are other gay professors," I said.

"Yeah, but how easy do you think it is for any of them?"

"Why should it be any harder for them now? Nobody cares if you're gay anymore; I mean, nobody except parents and Bible Belt types."

Zoe sniffed in a more than merely contemptuous way. She sounded as though she was about to cry and her nose had decided to join in too. "Keith, you are incredibly naïve."

"Well, then if they don't want her because she's gay, then maybe it's already decided and you don't enter into it."

"Keith, they can't openly refuse her for being gay! They'll use me as an excuse. They'll say she's corrupting her students, or something like that."

At this point a weedy-looking sort with a long black ponytail, a gauzy orange outfit that appeared to have been dyed in his home washing machine, and wooden beads that resembled a rosary but were emphatically not Catholic, approached us with a most disapproving expression and hissed "Could you please keep your voices down in the library?" He did not wait for our reply.

"The hell with this," said Zoe, "I might as well go."

"Me too," I said, abandoning my periodicals. "I think I'm done studying. Do you want to go to the coffee shop and get something?"

"No, I just want to get out," said Zoe. "Life is just hell. Columbus should never have discovered the New World; then I would never have been born."

I was not sure there was anything I wanted to say to that, so we descended the stairs to the main level in silence, allowed the student guarding the exit to examine our backpacks, and went out the wide glass doors onto the patio. As if by one pair of feet, we crossed to the rail that prevented us from leaping or falling into the lower-level study garden, and stared down into the planters. After a moment, I said "Are you going to be all right?"

"No," said Zoe, "and there's nothing you can do about it."

19

After leaving Zoe, who had no intention of going back to her room, I walked aimlessly awhile under the trees, contemplating her situation. I had no real objection to her relationship with Lina Troyer; I considered it unwise, but if pressed I would not have been able to say that any romantic attachment was wise or safe to embark on, and this belief had neither prevented me from my own entanglements, nor caused me to censure those of others. How, after all, could any student be wise to distract him- or herself with so tumultuous an undertaking as falling in love? But we all seemed prey to this sort of thing from time to time, whether from some biological imperative—by which I do **not** refer to the reproductive instinct—or from social conditioning, or even from the historical fact of being at the tag-ends of Western Civilization and having inherited that which Denis de Rougemont considered a medieval innovation and perversion, "romantic love."

Romantic love, indeed. Once the specter of de Rougemont and his celebrated book invaded my thoughts, I was constrained to wonder whether Zoe Vogel and Lina Troyer recognized their attachment as belonging in that tradition of pain, worship, and renunciation, or whether they felt as lesbian Marxists that that model had been long superseded. Did they believe that the love of which the troubadours sang was purely the neurosis (or pinnacle) of a feudal society? Did they believe that that style of love had been supplanted by a bourgeois variety, and that there was now some new kind attained by lesbian Marxist intellectuals? Or did they believe, as I did, that the notion of romantic love has existed without fundamental alteration over the centuries, despite the persistence and occasional birth of other approaches?

I was inclined to think that, no matter what Zoe and her beloved might aspire to in the realms of equality, honesty, and avoidance of male stereotypes, the existence of Zoe's worship of Lina, her apparent willingness to renounce something (even if she was not sure what) to benefit her lover, and the obvious pain that she suffered, all indicated that she fell into the traditional category of a romantic lover.

None of this, of course, was of any use in assuaging her feelings. Nor, indeed, was it likely to assist Lina Troyer in obtaining tenure. In fact, it was not even of any help in solving any of my own problems in life (few though I am relieved to say they are). It was purely academic, and so purely academic that I was inclined to want to throw stones in vexation. I am a scholar, or at least one by intent and training, but I had never found scholarly work or methods to provide more than an anesthetizing influence on the emotions. If one is lucky, work provides an anodyne to pain; if not, then pain precludes all work.

On stumps to the right of my path, three squirrels skittered about, their tails bobbing. I decided that it was time to return to my room and read something appropriately infantile, or at least something that did not deal with love.

Consequently, after an hour or so of immersion in Edward Eager's **Half Magic,** I was refreshed and ready to tackle whatever the dining room might offer. I knocked on Tricia's door and found her simultaneously engaged in reading art history and gluing pictures of Deborah Harry and Joey Ramone into her datebook. Unlike Holly's business-like and much-penciled book,

Tricia's datebook is primarily an excuse to make collages of punk rockers, and its written portion is limited to occasional notes of "Anthro Section—10:30" and "Elvis Costello tickets go on sale;" and, from time to time when her favorite folk singers tour, the likes of "Martin Carthy comes to town!!! yaaay!!!!" Her interest in Italian Renaissance painters clearly flagging in the late afternoon despite the full-color Botticellis in front of her, Tricia greeted my mention of food with enthusiasm.

"I'm starving," she proclaimed. "Is it really 5:30 already?"

I assured her that it was.

"I wonder what they're having," she went on. "Do you remember what they had on the menu?"

"No." I do not usually memorize our dining room's upcoming attractions; they are not so exciting that I would wish to fantasize about them in advance.

Tricia began to rummage through her pockets. "Darn, what've I done with my meal card?" Since it was affixed to her reg card, and since Tricia's desk is always strangely tidy for that of an Art major, I could not imagine that the meal card could have gone far. And indeed, it had not. No sooner had I turned to look at the Pretenders poster next to the wardrobe, than Tricia had found her meal card in a jacket pocket, and a gathering of other Hall members had arrived behind me.

After the usual milling around in front of Tricia's door, we went on to join the line to the dining room, where we were disappointed to find that hamburgers awaited us. Or, more specifically, a choice between hamburgers, cheeseburgers, meatloaf, and a nasty-looking vegetarian offering that consisted of some sort of casserole with lumps of tofu. Confronted with this unexciting fare, we opted as one for the cheeseburgers, and expressed our individuality at the salad bar and in our choice of cottage cheese or Jello.

We found a table and set down our trays.

"Oh **really,**" exclaimed Holly suddenly. She had been reading—or more accurately, flipping through—a newspaper.

"What?" said Carolyn.

"Look at this," replied Holly, shoving the paper under Carolyn's cheeseburger in time to catch a blob of ketchup.

"Why is it," said Carolyn to no one in particular, or perhaps directly to the gods, "why is it that only **my** food drips?"

"It isn't," said Tricia, with both reassurance and personal satisfaction as she viewed the minuscule grease spot on her own plate, "it's just that yours always drips more."

"**Read,**" said Holly, "don't drip." Holly's plate was also nearly devoid of splatters.

Carolyn took a bite out of the offending sector of her burger, whereupon a large dollop of mustard joined the ketchup on the newspaper.

"Ick," said Holly. "Are you reading or not?"

"Yes, I've read it," replied Carolyn. "It's stupid. Here, you can have it back."

"Yes, with hamburger condiments ..." said Holly.

"What are you reading?" I asked.

"The **Banner,**" said Carolyn scathingly.

"Another trite, uninformative article on Richard Gurney," said Holly.

"Oh, let me see!" exclaimed Tricia. Disregarding the splotches Carolyn had left on the paper, she took and scanned it eagerly.

"Well?" I prompted.

"Yeah, it's dumb all right," she said. "Listen:

INVESTIGATIONS CONTINUE

Local police continue to investigate the

inue to investigate the death of a man whose body was found on campus last weekend.

A spokesman said the man, 31-year-old Richard Gurney, was slain by an unknown assailant sometime Saturday afternoon or evening.

Gurney's body was discovered at 1:21 a.m. Sunday.

"Can't they come up with more than that?"

"Evidently not," said Holly. "You'd think ..." She did not bother to complete her sentence.

"One thing though," I said after taking a look at the paper myself. "They say he was killed 'sometime Saturday afternoon or evening.' Since they credit that to a 'spokesman,' the police must have done their autopsy."

"So?" said Holly.

"Yeah, what difference does it make if all they can say is that he died in the afternoon or evening?" said Carolyn.

"I didn't say it was of much use," I said, "but it's something we didn't know before."

"We could've guessed," said Tricia.

"After all, he didn't smell yet," said Carolyn.

"How do you know he didn't smell?" I said. "He was in the trash closet."

"He didn't smell enough to notice," said Holly, who is proud of her nose.

"Oh. Well, that's true," I admitted. "But it's still of some use to know he wasn't killed in the morning. It narrows things down slightly."

"So slightly as to be of no importance at all," said Holly. Then she looked at her watch. "Oh, **damn,**" she said. "Six o'clock. D'you have your things, Carolyn?"

Apparently the two had theatrical business to take care of at six; to the accompaniment of

Tricia's reminder of JoAnne's movie night, they grabbed their trays and ran off.

"That was sudden," said Evan, arriving with his own tray and taking the chair vacated by Holly.

"Rehearsal, I guess," said Tricia. "What's for dessert?"

"I didn't notice," said Evan.

"I wonder if I should get seconds," she muttered, and wandered off to the kitchen to look.

"What's this mess Carolyn's left?" asked Evan, gesturing at the **Banner.** "Didn't her mother ever teach her to pick up after herself?"

"Holly's newspaper," I said. "There's a brief mention of the murder investigation. Apparently the police have determined Gurney was killed in the afternoon or evening."

"How very precise," said Evan, glancing at the paper and then crumpling it up. "I don't know why Holly bothers to read the **Banner.**"

"I don't know why anybody does," I said. "Still ..."

"The cooking around here leaves something to be desired," announced Tricia upon her return with a second cheeseburger. "But—what the hey." She bit into this second wonder of culinary art, and then said "When are we going to go interview Dawnya Rankin?"

"Is she back yet?" said Evan.

"Who knows? Probably."

"We might as well talk to her after dinner," I said, "before she goes off to the movies, or to a dance, or wherever she normally goes on Friday night."

"That's assuming she's come back at all," said Tricia, taking another hefty bite out of her cheeseburger. "I mean, maybe she really never even made it to the Health Center. But we have to find out."

We finished our meal with no particular speed, as it seemed unlikely that we would find Dawnya Rankin in her room during dinner, but once we were on our way back to the dorm, our excitement began to increase. Soon we would probably meet Dawnya Rankin, the woman who had a clue so vital that the police had come to question her! Our speculations as to the nature of her knowledge ran rampant again, and Tricia hopped up and down rather like Liz's rabbit, chortling "Ho-ho! Hee-hee!" and merrily singing "We're off to see the Witness, the wonderful Witness of All!"

Since Tricia's singing and dancing is one of her usual responses to any form of excitement, no matter how trivial, Evan and I paid no attention, especially since upon leaving our Hall she switched to a tiptoe of exaggerated stealth that lasted past the stairs and Steve Madison's room to the entrance of the next Hall. Then she resumed her normal gait and we continued to Dawnya Rankin's door.

We stood for a second, and then Evan gave a brisk knock.

"Who's there?" came a voice from inside.

"We're from the next Hall," said Tricia as the door opened slowly and a large woman with cornrowed hair showed herself. "Are you Dawnya Rankin?"

20

"No, I'm **not** Dawnya Rankin," said the woman in the doorway, her accent faintly Southern. "I'm her roommate. What do you want with Dawnya?"

"We wanted to ask her something," said Tricia, faltering slightly. We had not imagined that Dawnya would be under guard.

"Well she's not in the mood to talk," said her protector. "She's not feeling well."

"It was our understanding that she knew something about Richard Gurney's murder," put in Evan. "Since we found the body, we—"

"What do they want?" said another voice from behind the door; a thin voice, which I assumed correctly to be that of Dawnya Rankin.

"Could we talk to you for a minute?" I inquired. "It's perfectly okay if your roommate stays," I added.

"What do you wanna do, Dawnya?" said the roommate over her shoulder, "there's three people here wanna talk to you about Richard Gurney."

"Oh," said Dawnya listlessly. She considered the idea, then said "Oh, I guess I can talk to them."

"Nobody says you **have** to," said her roommate.

"I might as well," said Dawnya.

The formidable roommate opened the door wide enough to let us pass, and we went in. Dawnya, a small pale girl with nearly albino uncombed hair, sat on her bed in an orange surfer-and-sunset T-shirt and gray sweats; she gestured for us to sit anywhere, so Evan and I pulled up the chairs and Tricia took the foot of the bed, while Nila Ross, the roommate, leaned against her own desk with crossed arms and a very skeptical expression.

"We found the body," said Tricia rapidly, "and that was pretty weird, so when we heard that you knew something about the murder, we decided to come over and ask you what it was."

"Oh," said Dawnya. She did not seem as though she was about to add anything more to this.

"Why do you want to know?" asked Nila.

"We'd like to get the whole thing cleared up so that people aren't afraid of getting killed," I said.

"Thought that was what the police were doing," said Nila.

"We do not doubt that they are," said Evan. "On the other hand ..."

"Since we found the body, we'd like to know as much as we can," said Tricia.

"I don't know why you want to talk to me, then," said Dawnya, hugging her knees to her chest.

"Dawnya doesn't know anything worth knowing about this murder," said Nila, "and what she does know, she already told the police."

"Well, what did you tell the police?" I asked of Dawnya. "It must've been **something.**"

Dawnya looked at Nila, then at us. "I told the police that I saw Richard Gurney in the trash closet about nine o'clock."

It seemed as though Evan, Tricia and I let out a mutual sigh at this news.

"Is that all?" said Evan somewhat tactlessly.

"Isn't that enough?" demanded Nila.

Dawnya began to cry. "It was awful! It was awful!" she moaned.

Tricia immediately moved over and put her arm around Dawnya. "It's okay," she said, while Nila said "Now look what you done, going and butting in like this. I knew you'd just upset her again, after the police and everything."

"It's all going to be okay," said Tricia, "the police'll catch whoever did it, and everything'll be fine."

Evan and I looked at the floor throughout this. Were we a bunch of insensitive louts that we had discovered the same body and suffered no particular anguish over it? Or was it simply that collective discovery of a body was less traumatic than discovering one alone?

"Why didn't you call the police at the time?" said Evan after a moment. "We didn't find the body till after midnight."

"I ... I don't know," said Dawnya, breaking down afresh.

"I think you people would do best to just go back to your own Hall and quit bothering Dawnya," said Nila. "I told you she didn't know anything worth knowing about this mess. There's no point in upsetting her any more."

Obliged to accept the truth of this, and naturally embarrassed at having caused a total stranger to burst into tears, we admitted that we were sorry to have upset Dawnya, expressed hope that she would feel better soon, and left.

"Omigod, how awful," said Tricia as we fled the scene. "I feel terrible. That poor girl."

"According to her account," said Evan, "she saw nothing worse than you did, and you aren't drooping around going into hysterics."

"I didn't look at him very closely," rejoined Tricia.

"Well, I did, and I'm not in tears," said Evan.

"That's different," said Tricia.

We entered our own Hall. "What's different?" said JoAnne, coming towards us with a film reel in each hand. "Look, Malcolm's got some great movies for us. I've never even heard of some of them, but he swears they're classics."

Just as willing to forget about our ill-fated interview with Dawnya, I looked at the titles on the film cans and saw **Un Chien andalou** and **The Fall of the House of Usher.**

"Classics," I agreed, "but rather unsettling ones." Buñuel's **Chien andalou** needs no introduction from me as a masterpiece of surrealism, while I recalled **The Fall of the House of Usher,** which I had seen some years back in a film history class, as a perhaps equally bizarre montage.

"Well, the popcorn popper's ready to go and I've got plenty of corn," said JoAnne cheerfully, "so once we get everything set up, it'll be movie madness."

She went back to the corner of the hall in which Holly and Carolyn had their rooms, where Malcolm was erecting the projector.

"Do you think Dawnya was telling the truth when she said all she saw was Richard Gurney sitting in the trash at nine o'clock?" inquired Evan.

I stopped short, and Tricia said "Of course she was!"

"How do you know?" said Evan. "You don't know her from Adam and Eve. She could be a pathological liar for all you know."

"But why wouldn't she tell the truth? I mean, assuming she's not a pathological liar."

"I noticed that that woman Nila was keeping a very careful eye on her," said Evan.

"That doesn't mean she's not telling the truth," said Tricia.

Holly and Carolyn entered, returning from the theater. "Who?" they said.

"We talked to Dawnya Rankin," I said.

"What, and you think she's a liar?" said Holly excitedly. "What'd she say?"

"All she said was that she saw Richard Gurney in the trash around nine," I said.

"But her roommate was keeping a close eye on her the whole time," said Evan. "I didn't get the idea that Dawnya Rankin was about to say anything her roommate didn't like."

"Wow," said Carolyn.

"Oh, Dawnya was just upset, and her roommate was looking out for her," said Tricia. "That's all it was. The poor girl started to cry when we asked her about the murder. You could tell she was feeling miserable."

"Oh," said Holly.

"That's **probably** all it was," I said.

"Nonetheless," said Evan, "it's entirely possible that there was something else. Or maybe that what she told us is a complete fiction. She seems to be under the roommate's thumb, and that could mean anything."

"She is not," said Tricia, "she's just upset."

"You just like to think the worst of people," said Holly. "I swear, I wish you'd all waited till I came back. Then we would've gotten some sense out of this."

"We did perfectly well as it was," I protested, "under the circumstances. It wasn't a situation where more questioners would have improved matters."

"Well, then I should have gone by myself," said Holly. "It sounds to me like you bungled the whole thing."

Carolyn sighed. "Why don't you tell us exactly what happened?"

This being a very sensible suggestion, we did just that; and by the end of the discussion, Holly was torn between belief in Evan's suspicions and Tricia's instincts, and Carolyn was of the opinion that we should ask Liz for further information on the characters and habits of Dawnya and Nila.

JoAnne approached. "Can I use one of your electrical outlets for the popcorn popper?" she inquired of Holly.

"Isn't there one in the corner?" said Holly impatiently.

"No," said JoAnne. It is my belief that she has not yet divined Holly's lack of enchantment with her, and that she assumes Holly is as well-disposed towards her as any of her other hall-members.

"Oh, all right," said Holly, rolling her eyes, "we'll use mine then."

The two went around the corner and could soon be heard moving the projector in order to open Holly's door; the blockage of the door would undoubtedly add to Holly's annoyance with JoAnne, but was unlikely to mar her friendship with Malcolm, the person who had put it there in the first place.

It might be as well at this juncture to mention one of the architectural peculiarities of our Hall, lest the reader take the word Hall to its logical conclusion, form a mistaken image of its shape, and thus be confused at the disappearance of Holly and JoAnne around a corner. For although one normally imagines a hall or corridor to be more or less straight, such a notion was evidently foreign to the person or persons who designed our dormitory. In actual fact, there is not a straight hallway in the building, unless perhaps in our very Hall; as a rule the corridors veer at unexpected angles from one another, and a Hall may have as many kinks as the pipe under a sink. This may, in fact, be part of the explanation why the neighboring Hall is so internally asocial, while ours is close: the other Hall is a long tunnel divided by an odd jog (very much as if an earthquake had moved half of it to one side), but ours is ring-shaped, with the bathroom and the phone alcove in the center.

Consequently, although none of our doors face other bedrooms, they all open to the center, and we are always meeting one another going back and forth. Of course, there is also the small matter that we have some collective clout with Theo Roth, and thus have a degree of choice as to who lives here.

"Okay, it's movie time," said JoAnne suddenly, emerging from Holly's room. "Get your pillows and cushions—fourth floor'll be coming down any minute."

Having forgotten—had I ever known—that fourth floor was to be included in the evening's entertainment, I hastily went to my room to get a pillow. The hall is not wide, and although I could see that Malcolm and JoAnne had lined it with a couch and some chairs, there would not be much room for two floors of Quiet Hall to sit between the projector and that blank wall beside my door at which the movies would be aimed.

As I unlocked my door, my eye was caught by a folded sheet of notebook paper tacked to my message board. My curiosity piqued at the privacy of the note (generally people scribble quite publicly on my notepad) and the fact that my name was not in Tricia's writing (for she will occasionally indulge a desire for mystery in this manner), I untacked the note and was about to turn on the light and read it, when I heard her say "But JoAnne, what did you **really** think of Richard Gurney?"

Forgetting the note, I grabbed my pillow and returned to the hallway to listen.

21

"Oh," said JoAnne, "he was okay, I guess. I mean, I didn't exactly pay a lot of attention to him."

"Why not?" demanded Holly.

"Well, I didn't really need his help planning anything, and his ideas were always kind of dumb," said JoAnne, reiterating the attitudes we ourselves had previously expressed.

"What kind of dumb ideas did he have?" I inquired.

JoAnne thought for a moment. "I don't know if they were actually dumb," she said; "I have a feeling that they just sounded that way coming from **him.** I mean, if somebody else had suggested them they might've sounded perfectly good. But somehow we could never get up much enthusiasm for any of his ideas. Like those sherry parties. If somebody else had come up with them, I might've thought they were a pretty neat idea. Sort of old-world and formal. But as it was I just thought it was kind of dopey, only I had to sound like it was special when I told people about it."

"I didn't get the impression there was anything old-world or formal about his sherry parties," said Evan. "According to Liz MacKellar, they were an excuse for him to get drunk and make advances to students."

I looked at Evan in some surprise. "That wasn't exactly the way she put it," I said.

"No? It was certainly the idea I got listening to her."

"Well, it's true she said he tried to get it on with Zoe Vogel, but that was only one incident."

JoAnne, meanwhile, had settled herself comfortably on the couch. "I hadn't heard about this business with Zoe Vogel," she said, "but it fits. Maybe he didn't actually have the parties in order to make advances to students—after all, the preceptors are supposed to have events that bring their Halls together—but I think he did tend to use them that way. There were three sherry parties, remember, and the invitees to each were a mixture of all his Halls—and it seems like I heard rumors that he came on to women at them. I mean, I didn't get any complaints, and neither did the other RAs, but word kind of went around that he was a little flirtatious." She paused and looked at the ceiling for a moment. "I felt like I had to go to the party I was invited to," she went on, "since I'm the RA and I'm supposed to set a so-called good example, and there was no question that he had his eye on one of the women there. I mean, he'd put his arm around her, and touch her when he walked by. Nothing intense; that is, she didn't seem to mind, so I didn't pay much attention at the time."

"Who was it?" asked Carolyn. By now we were all ensconced in the sofa and chairs, except for Malcolm, who was standing beside the projector, and except for the people from fourth floor, whose absence was probably due to the hour not yet having struck nine. JoAnne was proving to know at least a little about Richard Gurney, and I hoped that her information would not be interrupted by the fourth floor's arrival.

"It wasn't anyone I knew," she admitted. "Just some skinny kid I've seen on the stairs. I don't know if they ever got together or if she decided against it after I left."

Evan looked disgusted. "One would hope that this girl, whoever she was, would have had better sense ..."

"What a sleaze," said Tricia. "I bet she turned him down. I mean, why would anybody want to go to bed with Richard Gurney?" She stopped suddenly and added "Well, if they knew anything about him."

"Why?" said JoAnne, "was there something about him to know?"

"He was a sleaze," said Tricia.

"Yeah, but a pretty ordinary one," said JoAnne. "Plenty of sleazy guys manage to get women right and left; same for sleazy women. Besides, are we judging this on how many people they've fucked, or what?"

"Not exactly on that," said Holly authoritatively, "you can be so sleazy nobody'll sleep with you, or—well, Tamsin Gregory must've slept with half the male population, and she's not a sleaze, she's a nymphomaniac who happens to be a very nice person."

Evan's look of disgust having further deepened, he remarked "Thank you very much for the elucidation. I shall make a point of avoiding Tamsin's advances."

Tamsin was an extremely attractive, though not strictly beautiful, inhabitant of our dorm. Although I was not well acquainted with her, I had always heard that she was both a talented actress and a good listener. Whether her talent and responsiveness carried through to her erotic adventures I did not know, but her boyfriend seemed to be quite attached to her no matter what she did.

However, Tamsin Gregory was not, I felt, germane to our inquiries, and now the inhabitants of fourth floor were beginning to wander in.

"Hey, no fair, you guys've got all the best seats," they claimed, swarming cheerfully around us. "Surrender a cushion or two, okay?"

We shuffled around to permit them some room, and JoAnne extricated herself from the grip of the sofa in order to turn off the lights.

"The first movie on tonight's program," announced Malcolm, "will be the celebrated Buñuel-Dalí collaboration, **Un Chien andalou.** For those of you who haven't seen it before, viewer discretion is advised."

Obviously he referred to the famous razor-and-eyeball sequence; having seen it before myself, I was more interested to observe the rest of the audience than to improve my familiarity with the frame-by-frame details.

I was not surprised at the response: Tricia and JoAnne were heard to mutter "Eyeww," at the eyeball scene, while Holly and Carolyn maintained a stoic silence befitting their self-image as sophisticated theater majors. Had the film been one of no critical acclaim, they would have made as much noise as anyone, but they were in awe of

Buñuel and Dalí even if they did scorn the excesses of the early Roman dramatists.

Chien andalou, with its eyeballs, armpits, and ants, was soon over, and the lights went briefly on so that Malcolm could change reels. Carolyn disappeared into her room for tequila and was obliged to sit on Holly's lap upon her return due to the shifting of bodies on the couch, but other than this the evening moved smoothly on to **The Fall of the House of Usher.**

As the credits went by, I was surprised to note that it was directed by the French experimental filmmaker Jean Epstein; somehow I had been under the impression that it had been a product of Watson and Webber, a couple of Americans who I understood to have achieved nothing further of note (unless one counted their forays into homosexual erotica, a field that I suppose was not much explored in their day). Puzzled by the imperfection of my memory, I spent the majority of the film racking my brains as to why I should have confused the relatively prolific and respected Epstein with the creators of **Lot in Sodom.** Had it merely been that my instructor had lectured on Watson and Webber the same day as he had shown the Epstein film? Or had he said that Watson and Webber had also attempted a version of the Poe story?[1] I realized it was foolish of me to worry about that when I could be paying full attention to such superb and unusual cinematography, but Malcolm's choice was not in vain: it was a distinct hit with Carolyn, who was greatly impressed with its combination of slow motion, multiple superimposition, and intercut negative images.

The French silent short **Menilmontant** followed, with its almost equally strange and haunting story of two young women in the Paris slums and the apparent murder of one (I began to wonder exactly what had motivated Malcolm's selections), and then Chris Marker's foray into storytelling, **La Jetée.**

"Whoa!" exclaimed JoAnne after this was done and Malcolm was rewinding. "You picked some strange ones, but they were good!"

"Yeah," agreed several other voices. "Very bizarre. We should do this again."

In truth, the selection had been such that popcorn consumption had dropped markedly after the first, pre-showing, handfuls. I suspected that JoAnne had been expecting Clara Bow and Buster Keaton. Now, however, we all dug into the popcorn with enthusiasm, and the fourth-floor residents had just begun to ask us about finding Richard Gurney when Relief Proctor Sally appeared.

"Hey, Sally," cried JoAnne, "you just missed some great movies, but we've still got popcorn." She shook the bowl in Sally's direction.

"Thanks," said Sally, stepping over some legs and taking a handful. Somehow there was always something mildly comic about the sight of Sally, with her long unruly dishwater-blonde hair and friendly, wholesome face, along with her invariable flannel shirt, down vest, hiking boots, and belted walkie-talkie. Was it her job and the walkie-talkie, or just her build, that gave her the ponderous step of a cop?

"We were just talking about Richard Gurney," said one of the fourth-floor people. "Were you in on that too?"

Sally leaned against the wall and began to munch her popcorn. "No, not really. It's too bad I didn't notice something earlier and avoid you guys having to discover the body. I don't suppose I could've prevented the murder—I didn't hear about any fights or anything when I came on duty, and the only calls I got all night were one about a vagrant sleeping in a lounge, and one to tell the party in Holland House to keep the noise down. It seemed like a pretty dull night at the time, except for the hamster wake." She stopped and devoured some more popcorn.

"A vagrant?" said Holly. "Where was this vagrant? Maybe he did it."

"Well," said Sally, "actually he was in the lounge right over there—" she gestured in the direction of the stairs and the trash closet—"you know, the next Hall's lounge." There was a collective holding of breath, but Sally went on to say "Only, I got the call when I first came on duty, and whoever it was had split by the time I got there."

"The vagrant did it," said several voices, all with a soupçon of disappointment.

"Not necessarily," said Sally.

"What do you mean, not necessarily?" said Holly. "Isn't it obvious? Somebody reported the vagrant to Gurney before you came on duty, Gurney came upstairs to boot him out, and in the confrontation the vagrant attacked. Gurney got killed, the vagrant panicked and put him in the trash, and then the vagrant got himself out of here as fast as he could. He was probably some freaked-out Viet Nam vet who learned hand-to-hand combat in the army." She sighed. "It's utterly obvious. Now we know what the police are doing; they're rounding up all the transients downtown."

It was clear from Holly's expression that she was sorry that Richard Gurney should have died as a result of doing his job rather than for his sins. Evidently she favored the theory of divine retribution.

"No, not necessarily," said Sally again. "The police were interested in the vagrant, but they didn't seem convinced that he'd done the murder."

"Why not?" asked Tricia.

"Well, for one thing, if someone reports a vagrant and one of us goes to boot the guy out, usu-

ally the student comes along. Not always, and they don't usually want to be right on the scene," said Sally, taking another handful of popcorn, "but there's usually a little crowd hanging around somewhere nearby to find out what happens."

"Oh, come now, Sally," said Evan, "half the time when we report a vagrant no one shows up for hours."

Sally licked the salt from her fingers. "Too often, I agree, but then usually it turns out the vagrant is just somebody's visiting boyfriend. Anyway, I talked to the woman who reported this one, and she said she hadn't told Richard about it."

"Well, then obviously someone else did," said Holly.

"Not necessarily," said Sally yet again.

"You keep saying 'not necessarily,'" I said. "What makes you think the vagrant didn't do it?"

"Well, I've been thinking about it," said Sally, "I've been thinking about it a lot. And I know that the police took samples from the couch where the vagrant was supposedly sleeping—"

"When did they do that?" demanded Evan.

"Right after they'd talked to me," said Sally. "So I know they took samples, and I also know that the vagrant had medium-blond hair just like Richard Gurney, so—"

"Omigod!" burst out Tricia.

"I think this so-called vagrant was Richard Gurney," finished Sally.

---

1. Curiously enough, both Epstein and Watson *and* Webber brought out films of *The House of Usher* in 1928!

22

Our astonishment at hearing Sally's news was considerable. The fourth-floor residents, less well-informed to begin with, were especially startled, but even those of us who had been pursuing our own investigation were surprised.

"The blanket lint!" exclaimed Holly. "It fits right in!"

"Blanket lint?" said Malcolm.

"What blanket lint?" said JoAnne.

"The blanket lint that Officer Denny said was found on the body, of course." Realizing that not everyone present had heard of the blanket lint, or even of Officer Denny, Holly went on. "If somebody reported a vagrant sleeping in the lounge, they probably didn't look too closely in case he woke up."

"And vagrants usually sleep in blankets," said Carolyn helpfully.

"Right, and if it was Richard Gurney, the murderer must've just wrapped him in the blanket in order to carry him more easily. Or maybe the woman who reported the vagrant was really the murderer."

Everybody began to talk at once upon hearing these possibilities.

"Who reported the vagrant?" inquired Evan of Sally.

"Renee Gibeau," she replied. "Apparently she went to the lounge to study after dinner and found him there."

I tried to remember what I knew of Renee; surely I knew more than what little I must have heard from Liz. Then I remembered the long, smooth dark hair, the clean and well-fitting old Levi's, and the quiet air of unusual composure. I had met Renee Gibeau in Theo Roth's office, and she had been asking that Zoe Vogel's request to move be granted.

There had been nothing untoward about Renee, nothing out of place; certainly nothing suspicious. She had appeared cool, collected, and efficient; cool especially in her conversation with me, but not to the point of coldness. She had simply treated me as a stranger, and a stranger with whom she had no reason to dally.

But had she known that the sleeping vagrant in the lounge was really the corpse of Richard Gurney? Had she been a murderer coolly reporting his death?

I granted that this was possible, but I did not really think it was true. Renee Gibeau did not strike me as a likely murderer; she struck me as someone who usually minded her own business, who upon seeing a vagrant sleeping in the lounge would discreetly withdraw and call the appropriate authorities.

All the same, I knew almost nothing about her beyond her appearance, demeanor, and place of residence. For all I knew, she was the female serial killer who would refute Holly's half-baked theory that all serial killers were men.

"Was this right after dinner?" I asked idly.

"No, more like eight o'clock," said Sally. "It was the first thing I heard when I came on duty that night."

"So the body was moved between eight and 9:30," said Holly.

"9:30?" asked one of the fourth-floor people. "I thought you found him after midnight."

"The sign was on the door by then," explained Tricia, leaving the fourth-floor people just as confused as before.

"Could've been after eight," said Sally. "I didn't get there till about 8:30 since it wasn't urgent and I had to read Hank's log."

Hank was the weekday proctor, an elderly but much-beloved gentleman who had been known to assist us in many unorthodox but harmless endeavors. There had been, for instance, the time when he told us that there had been too many complaints of noise for us to continue a party in its original location, but that he would unlock one of the rooms off the dining area for us.

Sally took another handful of popcorn and apprised us of her need to continue her rounds. "But don't forget," she added, "the man on the couch may have been a perfectly real transient. Just because he had blond hair and might've been Richard Gurney doesn't mean he wasn't really just an ordinary bum."

She departed, walkie-talkie crackling, and the rest of us continued our discussion of the murder with renewed excitement.

Evan said, "If Sally is correct in taking the vagrant to be Richard Gurney, it is strange that his body should be found not in the lounge but in the trash closet."

"He came back to life and walked," said Carolyn, imbibing further tequila.

"Maybe the murderer was resting after carrying him that far," said Tricia.

"Well, but then why not just leave him there?" I inquired. "Why should it make any difference where he was found, so long as it wasn't in the killer's bedroom?"

No one appeared to have an answer for this.

"Do you think this Renee Gibeau woman who reported the vagrant might be the murderer?" asked JoAnne.

"Renee wouldn't kill anyone!" said Tricia, shocked. Then she tempered this with "I mean, I can't imagine why she would. Shit, I borrow her anthro book all the time."

"Just because one does not like to think an acquaintance would do such a thing ..." began Evan.

"This whole idea of Gurney being the vagrant throws a big monkey wrench in everything," complained Holly. "We don't know if he **was** the vagrant or if he was killed by one, Then, if he **was** the vagrant, we don't know whether Renee killed him or just reported him. **And,** if Renee killed him, why did he end up in the trash?"

"I don't think Renee killed him," said Carolyn. "If she had, it'd be stupid of her to put him in the trash after reporting he was in the lounge. That is, unless someone else moved him."

"Don't be silly, who'd move a body they didn't kill?" said Holly, adding "but it's silly to think Renee killed him anyway, because she could never've carried him even to the lounge."

"She could've killed him right there," said JoAnne, "and just put the blanket over him so he'd look like a vagrant."

"But then why put him in the trash?" said Tricia, while Malcolm said "I really don't see why we should suspect Renee of killing Richard Gurney just because she reported seeing a transient sleeping in the lounge."

"Yeah, I thought we were suspecting Ferdinand," said Tricia.

This remark caused even more of a stir.

"Ferdinand?" cried JoAnne and the fourth-floor residents avidly. "Why Ferdinand?" Their questions multiplied as if by some logarithmic formula.

"Did he do something suspicious?"

"Do you have any clues pointing to him?

"Did he and Richard have a fight?"

And, again, "Why Ferdinand?"

We answered these questions as best we could, until finally, curiosity mostly satisfied, people began to drift back upstairs. Malcolm rolled the projector into his room for the night, Carolyn brought forth her bottle of tequila, and those of us remaining settled back onto the couch to contemplate the events of the past week. At around midnight, Pauline joined us, but paid little attention to our news that the body might have lain in the lounge.

"I need to think," she announced gravely, perching herself on the back of the couch and gazing darkly at the wall across from her, her chin in her hands and her elbows on her knees. She looked slightly spooky like this, but we were familiar with her fey moods and paid little atten-tion.

In the morning I awoke to the faint sounds of what has been called "that damned cheerful folk music" wafting from Carolyn's window. While I would not tune in to any of it by choice, I have never objected to an occasional dose of it, even in the morning. And, assured by my faithful Tintin clock that the hour was a respectable 9:30 and that I need neither leap up and run to brunch nor wonder how I would survive until the opening of the kitchen, I lay in the pleasant sunlight of my uncurtained window and listened to Carolyn's matutinal choices.

First came a bouncy French number about a young man who somehow broke his leg as a result of an admirer dropping an orange on the limb. As if this were not surprising enough, the ensuing verses indicated that his doctor chose to amputate.

As I gazed at the ceiling pondering the mind required to invent such a lyric, Carolyn changed the record in favor of one featuring a ballad about a rather different youth, this time one whose mother encouraged him to kill his beloved in return for a new shirt and some pocket money. This one went on at great length, and I was alarmed to note that the boy took his mother up on the offer. Feeling that such a song was really not appropriate to Saturday-morning lounging, I got out of bed only to hear Carolyn put on a version of "Lord Randal," that well-known lament of a man poisoned by his lover.

Worse and worse, I thought. Why couldn't we listen to innocuous songs about kings or highwaymen or lost cities or whatever else these people normally sang about; or the Peruvian harp music or Baroque chamber music that Carolyn also fancied? Why must we be assailed with songs about amputation and murder?

With this in mind, I threw on my clothes and went out to the bathroom to wash. Luckily, Carolyn's music was substantially muffled by her closed door, and obliterated by the rush of water from the tap.

At brunch some time later, I loaded up my tray with oatmeal and bacon, and located Evan, who was devouring a plate of eggs.

"I thought you were adhering to Chong's diet," I commented.

"I'm not sure that's possible around here," he said—a conclusion I had long ago reached—"and besides, who knows if it works? Either he's right or he's crazy."

"True," I said. I was not, however, so interested in the efficacy of Chong's diet as in this indication that Evan was beginning to turn from Chong's teachings as he had turned from his various choices of major. Would this be a brief period of doubt, or would he soon be devoting his energies to pointing out the weaknesses of Chong's entire method? I had always been perfectly content with the practical aspect of the class; I had little desire to listen to Evan attempt to persuade me to drop it. However, perhaps matters would not come to that. Perhaps I was thinking too much of past experience.

Carolyn joined us with a plate of French toast, and then Holly with the same, but, predictably, they had no opinions to contribute on Chong's diet. After some minutes, during which time Carolyn departed and returned with coffee, Pauline and Tricia approached, talking excitedly about something or other. Pauline seemed to be doing most of the talking, but at intervals Tricia would exclaim and only refrained with difficulty from wild gesticulations. It was this, in fact, which caught my attention: I was curious whether she would drop her tray before reaching the table.

She did in fact spill some of her milk, which was unusual enough for Tricia, but once she had parked her tray securely on the table and started to shovel in a heaping bowl of grits, my attention went back to Evan and his developing dissertation on Chong's diet.

"There is no scientific basis for a strict macrobiotic diet or any variation thereof," he was saying, "and Chong's diet is ..."

I listened politely in order to nod my head and insert the proper yeses and noes, but beyond this my mind was not deeply engaged.

"Astrid said **what?**" I heard Carolyn exclaim, but missed the answer.

"Brown rice and distilled water are all very well," said Evan persuasively, thumping a finger on the table in case I had missed this vital point, "but ..."

"Why would they do that?" Holly was saying.

"Because they're fucking lunatics!" said Pauline shrilly.

I wondered who the lunatics in question were; probably the Art Department. Then Carolyn said

"You don't know how bizarre they are, Holly. They'd do just about anything."

She paused, and Evan said something about the virtues of soy milk. She then went on to say something about "... were in the same mask-making class last year. I swear they spent the whole class standing there groping each other."

This was followed by an unintelligible series of exclamations and opinions, overlaid by the potassium content of bananas and whether Chong was correct in excluding them from his diet.

"... final project was a mask with a big dick hanging off the forehead covered with thumbtacks and straight pins and about four colors of Jackson Pollock," concluded Carolyn disdainfully.

I decided that their conversation did not refer to the Art Department.

"Do you think we should investigate fencing next quarter?" asked Evan.

"I think we should call the police," said Holly.

23

Call the police? What did a phallic mask bedizened with pins and paint splotches have to do with the police?

I refrained from making any sudden movements, and gestured unobtrusively for Evan to be silent; after all, this might prove to be one of those mysterious topics from which we were being excluded.

"I thought of that," Pauline was saying, "but what's the use? It'll just piss them off and what'll the police do anyway?"

"That's silly," said Tricia, "if they did it, they shouldn't get away with it. I think that was a really sick thing to do."

Evan and I exchanged puzzled glances. Surely the Gang of Four could not be debating whether to turn in the murderer! Or murderers, as it sounded. Really, this could not be. They must be discussing something else, something related to mask-making and people who displayed the bad taste to grope one another during lectures.

Either way, I was anxious to learn what it was all about.

"They sound like total weirdos from everything I've heard," said Holly. "It's beyond me what any of you see in them. I think we should call the police right away and get it over with."

"I suppose," said Pauline, "but I want to talk to them first."

"Talk to them!" said Holly. "What **for?** So they can do something creepy to you?"

"They wouldn't do anything creepy to me," said Pauline staunchly. "I just think I should let them know we're going to call the cops. After all, they're my friends."

"You must be crazy," said Holly. "I notice this Astrid woman didn't sic the police on them, she just made a point of leaking you the information so she wouldn't have to be involved."

"They won't do anything to me," insisted Pauline. "They'll just laugh, like they always do."

"Yeah, that's probably true," said Carolyn. "They're not violent, they just have their own psychotic outlook on life."

"They're just always on drugs," said Tricia.

"Great," said Holly. "Just splendid. I don't like it one bit. So listen to me, Pauline Young, if you think you're going to tell them that we're calling the police, we are **all** going to tell them."

The Gang of Four began to push back its collective chairs.

"I'm not going to let you out of my sight until this is over," said Holly.

Realizing that they were about to leave the table without our having discovered what the unidentified persons on drugs had done, Evan and I too pushed back our chairs.

"What's going on?" I asked as we lined up to throw our trash and send our trays to the kitchen.

There was a pause, as they apparently mulled over whether to tell us. Fortunately it was not a long one; Tricia said "We found out who moved the body."

"Are you certain of this?" inquired Evan.

"Of course," said Carolyn.

"Gilbert and Lainey did it," added Tricia confidently. "Astrid told Pauline last night."

We began to walk up the stairs to the Quad, ignoring the late stragglers going the other direction. I brought to mind my knowledge of the notorious pair and did not find it altogether improbable that they might have moved a body. Lainey, I knew, was an Art major of statuesque proportions and laissez-faire attitudes; Gilbert was a madman, a party animal of indeterminate breed and unknown academic focus.

"Who is Astrid?" I asked as we crossed to Damson House.

"Gilbert's girlfriend," said Carolyn and Pauline.

"I was under the impression," said Evan, "that Lainey was Gilbert's girlfriend."

"Oh no," said Tricia, "they're just friends."

"They've been having an affair since at least last spring," said Carolyn, "but Astrid's still Gilbert's girlfriend."

"Hmm," I said. From what I had seen and heard of Gilbert, I was not sure why anyone at all would be attracted to him, but perhaps these women were simply fatally—or rather, I corrected myself, inexorably—drawn to men with raven hair and moronic laughs. "Isn't Astrid aware of his relationship with Lainey?" I went on to ask. "Or is that why she's telling everyone that he and Lainey moved the body?"

"Astrid doesn't mind about Lainey," said Pauline. "If she did, they'd've broken up a long time ago."

I did not ask whether she meant that Astrid would have broken up with Gilbert, or that Astrid would have made sure that Gilbert would have broken off with Lainey; I suspected that the emotional habits of all three were of an alien variety, as unpredictable as those of snakes or nematodes.

"Astrid told me because she didn't think they should've moved the body and she wasn't sure whether she ought to tell anyone about it."

"She seems to have told you," said Evan.

"She meant whether she should tell someone at the College Office," returned Pauline.

"Astrid thinks about that kind of thing," said Tricia.

"She looks after Gilbert," said Carolyn. "She probably writes all his papers so he doesn't flunk out."

Holly snorted. "I think we should just call the police and be done with it. If we do it now, the police'll get here while Gilbert and Lainey are still sleeping off whatever they did last night."

"No," insisted Pauline, "I have to talk to them first."

The six of us stood in the hallway next to the fire hose and its glass case, Pauline looking the picture of stubbornness.

"I already told you, Pauline," said Holly, "if you go we all go. I don't want them hitting you on the head or something."

"At least take me and Carolyn," said Tricia. "They know us."

"No," said Holly, "all of us. Keith and Evan, too. You don't know what they might do when you knock on the door, they might freak out."

Although I thought this a trifle unlikely, I was not about to say so for fear of missing out on what was sure to be both the most bizarre and the most informative confrontation yet.

"After all," said Holly, "maybe they didn't just move the body; maybe they killed him too."

With this, the entire unwieldy group of us headed down the hall towards Lainey's room.

"Now you guys hang back and position yourselves there," directed Holly, indicating that Evan and I were to stand in the stairwell around the corner from Lainey's door, "and we'll be right here behind Pauline."

"This is absurd," I muttered to Evan, but he had gotten himself into the spirit of Holly's little drama and was flattened against the concrete slab wall just like a television hero waiting to be shot at.

Pauline knocked. "Lainey?"

There was a faint sound of rustling and shuffling.

"Lainey? I need to talk to you and Gilbert."

"Coming." There was more rustling, and then a door opening. "Hey, Pauline! Whatcha doing? Hey, it must be morning! Gilbert, open the curtains, willya?"

Lainey Silver's voice was low and surprisingly mellifluous for a woman who allegedly spent all of her time doing drugs and wandering about nude; it was also unexpectedly friendly. Of course, I reminded myself, she did not yet know why Pauline was at her door.

"Whoa, not that far, Gilbert," she said, "I can't take that much light this early in the morning."

"It's **noon**," said Gilbert, "didja know that?" He sounded as though this were some sort of arcane private joke, and they both laughed.

"So what'd you want to see us about so early in the ... **noon** ... for?" said Lainey. "I'd invite you in, but you can see how it is." She laughed again.

It is difficult for me to imagine a room any untidier than Pauline's, but I have been assured that Lainey Silver's was at least in the running. According to Holly, the portion visible from the door was entirely filled with bedsheets, laundry, and colored pencils. Then Gilbert joined Lainey in the doorway, effectively blocking the view of the floor, but providing an informative one of the occupants.

According to Holly, Lainey had ambled naked to the door, and upon opening it had stood leaning on the frame like a figure from one of the more monumental late nineteenth-century bronzes—one representing sloth, or concupiscence, or something of that kind. She was neither fat nor what Holly was willing to term voluptuous, but simply large. She had dragged part of one of the bedsheets to the door with her, but rather than draping herself in it, she simply held it in the hand that she leaned on, so that it cascaded to the floor somewhat as her long, wavy, and uncombed brown hair cascaded into her eyes and over her shoulders.

Gilbert's arrival in the doorway was evidently equally unconventional: equally naked, he stood about a head shorter than Lainey without seeming any smaller. With another of his apparently motiveless laughs, he said "Hi, Pauline," in tones that struck me as obnoxious but which perhaps Lainey and Astrid found seductive, and put his arm around Lainey in order to be able to palpate her breast. Then, noting the presence of Tricia and Carolyn, he greeted them as well.

"I was talking to Astrid last night," announced Pauline, "and she told me that you moved the body."

This somehow struck Gilbert and Lainey as tremendously funny. They looked at each other in a way Carolyn terms "complicitous," and then Gilbert began to chuckle in a way I myself would call maniacal.

"What body," he said, "we never moved any body, did we?"

"Yeah, what body?" said Lainey.

They both went into gales of laughter, which Holly describes as disgusting and which caused Evan to tense, ready to spring at any moment kicking onto the scene like the aforementioned television hero.

Their laughter continued unabated until Gilbert paused to say "Of course we moved him, didn'tcha know we moved him?" Which merely set them off again.

"You shouldn't've moved him," said Pauline sternly. "That was really stupid."

"Yeah, you really shouldn't've moved him," said Tricia.

"If you hadn't moved him," said Pauline, "we wouldn't have to call the police."

Gilbert and Lainey looked at her.

"The police!" said Lainey. "Why do you wanna call the police?" She sounded mystified that anyone would consider doing such a thing.

"Come on, Pauline," said Gilbert suavely, "don't be a **drag.**"

"The cops're a drag," said Lainey, her voice just as attractive as it had been upon opening the door.

"You don't wanna be a **drag,** do you Pauline?" said Gilbert. "I hate it when you're such a drag."

Pauline, of course, was unaffected by this nonsense: once she makes up her mind on some moral issue, or even on something that she fancies to be a moral issue but which is in fact something she has invented on the basis of some misunderstanding or slight, she will not be swayed by any amount of argument. Only time and her own internal reassessment of a situation will change her mind once she has set a course; which means that when she does change her mind, her alteration is more baffling than either Evan's or Holly's changes, because she has done nothing to signal it in advance.

But there was no cause for Pauline to change her mind here; she simply said "Speak of drags ..."

"You don't know what a drag the cops are," said Lainey. "They just fuck everything up."

"I don't care what you think about the police," said Pauline. "I could've called them without telling you, but I thought you should know first." She took a breath. "If you're going to be **childish** about it"—being childish is a particular sin in Pauline's lexicon—"then that's just tough."

With that, she turned to go, the rest of the Gang of Four following.

"Wait, Pauline!" said Gilbert, "you don't **mean** it, do you?"

"You aren't **really** going to call the cops, are you?" said Lainey.

"I already told you what I'm going to do," said Pauline without turning around. "I don't have time for this kind of childish behavior, so **bugger off.**"

"Aw, Pauline," whined Gilbert, "we didn't mean any harm." Apparently he realized the seriousness of Pauline's "bugger off," a Britishism she reserves for the most loathsome of people. "It was a crackup, you shoulda been there. Really."

Pauline ignored him, and the Gang of Four disappeared down the hallway.

24

"What a drag," said Lainey.

"Yeah, what a drag," echoed Gilbert.

"I guess we better get ready to talk to the cops," Lainey went on.

"Yeah, total bummer," said Gilbert. "What a drag."

They then retreated into Lainey's room and closed the door without subjecting us to further verbal pyrotechnics.

"Well!" I said as Evan relaxed from his pose. He looked slightly disappointed at not having had an opportunity to practice the martial arts on Gilbert and Lainey.

"A most unappealing pair," he remarked as we abandoned the stairwell and headed after the Gang of Four.

"At least they don't seem to have any plans to escape," I said.

"Where would they go? They're not smart enough to think of a good escape."

It seemed to me that anyone with the brains to get into a good university must be smart enough to elude the police for a while, but it was just as well that Lainey and Gilbert seemed willing to eschew the possibility. Perhaps things would wind up rapidly now; for though I did not think Gilbert and Lainey had committed the murder, they might be able to provide further evidence when questioned.

When we reached our Hall, Pauline was in the phone alcove finishing her call to the police. We waited patiently as she repeated the particulars and hung up, but before we could ask for further details of Astrid's confession, Liz arrived with Hemingway on a leash.

"What a good bun-bun!" exclaimed Tricia, flinging herself to the floor in order to examine his harness and cosset him for his unaccustomed docility.

"You can undo his leash if you want," said Liz.

"He won't go far with his Aunt Tricia around to pet him," said the aunt in question; as predicted, Hemingway settled promptly into a mass of spotted fur. "Lovely bun-bun," she began to coo into his cocked ears. "Fat Hemmy-poo."

"I just found out something about Dawnya Rankin," announced Liz as she poked Hemingway affectionately with her toe.

"About Dawnya Rankin!" said Holly.

"We did interview her," Evan pointed out, adding "She was surprisingly upset considering she claimed only to have seen the body before we did."

"I know," said Liz. "In fact, I guess you could say that's exactly it."

"What?"

"Seeing the body, I mean," said Liz.

"Do you mean she didn't see it after all?" demanded Holly.

"No, no, she saw it," said Liz. "The point **is** that she saw it. I mean ... Well, I was talking to my RA after brunch, so I figured I'd ask her about Dawnya."

"Uh-huh," said Carolyn encouragingly.

"And Pam said that Dawnya was upset about finding the body, and about not having called the police, but she didn't know what to do about it, so finally she told Nila."

"Her roommate," said Evan, in case any of us had forgotten.

"Yes," said Liz. "And Nila told her to call the police, but she still didn't know if she wanted to do that and she was still freaked out, so after Nila got sick of arguing with her, **she** told Pam."

Tricia and Hemingway were still entangled on the floor, but I noticed that Tricia, if not Hemingway, was paying close attention to Liz's narrative.

Liz went on. "So Pam and Nila talked to her at great length, and she cried a lot and looked like she was going to go into hysterics" (I could well believe this), "but finally they got it out of her that the reason she didn't want to tell the police was that she'd slept with Richard Gurney and was afraid that they'd suspect her of the murder."

"Wow!" said Tricia, rolling away from Hemingway and sitting up.

"God!" said Carolyn.

"I swear," said Holly. "I knew I should've been there to talk to her."

"What else did she say?" I inquired.

"Dawnya, or Pam?"

"Both," said Evan.

"Well," said Liz, "I don't know if Dawnya said a whole lot else, but they persuaded her to tell the police, so she did, and after that she was still freaked out, so they decided they'd better take her over to the Health Center so she could be under observation for a while."

"I can't believe this," said Holly. "What kind of relationship did she have with Richard Gurney, anyway?"

Liz sighed. "Well, it sounds like he came on to her at one of his sherry parties, not the one I was at, but a different one, and she ended up spending the night. I don't know if there was any more to it than that, but it wasn't very long ago."

"Ick," said Holly succinctly. Carolyn crossed her arms and looked at the ceiling.

"Did your RA think Dawnya might have murdered him?" I asked.

Liz reached down to pet Hemingway. "I didn't ask, but I don't think so. I mean, why would

Dawnya kill him? If she decided she didn't like him after all, wouldn't she just go on with her life?"

"Well, that's what most people would do," I agreed. "But she seems to be extremely upset about the murder."

"Well, maybe she still liked him," said Liz. "She must've liked him enough to sleep with him. And it must be pretty weird to open the trash and find your lover sitting there dead, even if he's your ex, or even if you only slept with him once, or even if you didn't like him."

"True," I conceded.

"Obviously we'll simply have to talk to Dawnya Rankin again," said Evan. "But in the meantime other information has come to light."

"Yeah, that's right, you haven't heard!" said Tricia. "Pauline found out that Gilbert and Lainey moved the body from the lounge to the trash closet."

"Gilbert and Lainey?" queried Liz. "Why on earth would they do that?"

"Yes," said Evan to Pauline, "what **was** their reason? Or do they simply indulge in random illegal acts on a continual basis?"

"I don't think they had any special reason," said Carolyn.

"How could they possibly have any reason to shlep dead bodies around?" said Holly. "They're obviously out of their minds."

"According to Astrid," said Pauline, ignoring this largely justified attack on her friends, "they were wandering through the dorm waiting for the acid to take effect, but they stopped in the lounge to roll a joint on the table."

"With a dead body in the room?" exclaimed Liz; I suspected that this was precisely what Tricia had said on her way to brunch.

"I don't think they knew it was a dead body yet," said Pauline. "I think they just thought he was some dude asleep on the couch."

"Still ..." said Carolyn, whose precise attitude towards Lainey and Gilbert I had not yet fathomed.

Pauline shrugged. "Astrid said they stood on the balcony smoking the joint and then went back in to pick up their stash and tried to wake him up."

There was a short silence as we all imagined Gilbert and Lainey hollering "Hey man, wake up! Let's party!" or some such inanity.

"But," she continued, "since he didn't wake up, they decided to pick him up in his blanket and put him in the trash."

Again, we pictured Gilbert and Lainey in the lounge: perhaps shaking Gurney, or yelling "Come on, man, let's party!" in his unresponsive ear; we could hear them saying "Hey, let's dump him in the trash!" and "Hey, he's a heavy fucker!" as they laughingly carted him away.

"Well," said Liz after a moment, "that sounds pret-ty re-pul-sive to me."

"We called the police," offered Tricia.

"I would hope so!" said Liz, and I was reminded of the white cutwork and lace of her virginal bedroom, the stack of nineteenth-century novels upon the shelf. It seemed odd enough that she permitted—nay, encouraged—an insubordinate spotted rabbit into her life to pee on her pillows; surely the likes of Gilbert and Lainey were almost beyond her imagining. But then, I did not know Liz well.

"What did they do," she inquired, "run off and tell everyone that they'd just stuck a body in the trash closet?"

"No," said Pauline, "I don't think they told anyone but Astrid."

"Gilbert's girlfriend, right?"

"Yeah."

Astrid and Gilbert's relationship seemed to have remained public knowledge despite his affair with Lainey. It did seem odd to me, but if they were all happy with it, I hardly cared about that part of their lives.

"When they got to that party in Holland House, Astrid was already there, so they told her all about it."

"Very strange," said Liz. "Now if I were moving a body …" She stopped. "Hey, who put the sign on the door?"

I had totally forgotten about the sign. "Yeah, what about the sign?" I demanded.

"Astrid put it there," said Pauline. "She didn't think people should be opening the door and finding a body."

"Very sweet," said Evan dryly, "the sign of a hopelessly muddled mind. Instead of reporting the death, she puts a sign up in the hope that no one will notice the body until it putrefies."

"Ugh," said Holly, "do you have to be so graphic?"

"What else could she be hoping? Her mind clearly operates on a purely short-term basis."

"Well, I don't give a damn about Astrid's mind," I said, "other than to wonder how anyone could be attracted to Gilbert, but ..."

"God, the police should be showing up any minute!" Holly interrupted. "I wonder if they'll take 'em away."

"Yeah, I wonder," said Carolyn.

A great curiosity suddenly struck us as to how Lainey and Gilbert were faring with the police, and with little ado we were headed back through Liz's Hall—Liz having popped Hemingway onto her shoulder for greater speed—and towards Lainey's isolated room near the stairs.

A small crowd of other students had arrived before us, however, and were clustered around the narrow windows next to the stairs, and at the larger windows of the last rooms in the Hall.

We pushed our way towards the stairwell windows, and saw the police down in the parking lot putting Gilbert and Lainey into a black-and-white.

25

"I didn't really think they'd take them away," whispered Tricia, looking a little stricken and muddling her pronouns as a result. "I mean, it's not like they killed him or something."

"What did you think the police would do, pat them on the head and say it was okay?" said Evan with considerable asperity. "They're accessories after the fact, aren't they?"

Tricia said nothing, but I could understand that the excitement of calling the police was a thing far removed from the reality of seeing friends or acquaintances summarily hauled away. I felt that Gilbert and Lainey deserved whatever they might get, but all the same I did not think I would be anxious to bring in the police for much short of the actual murder.

"I think I'm going to go downtown," said Carolyn suddenly. "I want a break from all this death, especially when I've got rehearsals to deal with."

The other members of the Gang of Four agreed with this, and Holly and Tricia decided to join Carolyn on the bus downtown, while Pauline announced her intention to spend the remainder of the afternoon working on her canvas of Aunt Jemima and the Jolly Green Giant.

Evan, too, rapidly disappeared, and I was left facing the prospect of actual study. Realizing how little I looked forward to this, yet how useless further speculation about Richard Gurney would probably be, I became irked that a man I had not even liked should have succeeded in distracting me from my studies for an entire week.

I do not mind being distracted; I think it normal and rational that one should do something other than study eighteen hours a day. I have known many students who confess to a feeling of guilt should they catch themselves reading a book purely for pleasure, and I find them naïve and foolish. If they had not liked to read in the first place, was there any reason for them to attend a university? Even the most math-addicted of my acquaintances are fond of books.

And conversation: is there any fun in an existence devoid of friends and conversation? It is good to know the uses of solitude and to concentrate on one's work, but it is far better to be able to juggle solitude and companionship.

And even this foray into detection was interesting and from time to time exciting. It was certainly not a thing that had previously come my way in six years of undergraduate life.

No, I do not mind being distracted; but I was a little perturbed that Richard Gurney had done it so thoroughly.

And with that thought in mind, I plunged firmly into my books.

By five o'clock I was feeling both virtuous and ravenous. I had caught up with my reading in two of my classes and had jotted down some notes for a paper in the third; I had washed the ink stains from my Formica desk-top; and, although I had consumed an entire bottle of Vernor's ginger ale, I was hungry enough to eat whatever the kitchen offered.

Almost. Mine is not a sensitive stomach, but I had learned not to be too careless in the matter of dormitory food.

Fortunately, as I stood in line reading the mail that I had neglected to retrieve after brunch, the kitchen was advertising eggplant parmesan. And, although eggplant by itself is not a vegetable that I altogether approve of, the college's eggplant parmesan is quite palatable, much more so than was my mail.

For, in addition to the usual junk mail that afflicts even dorm-dwellers (entreating me to buy subscriptions to Christian youth periodicals; begging me to support my incumbent congressman in his bid for re-election; wheedling me to send away for records that I need only pay for if kept), there was a letter from my parents craving to know when, if ever, I planned to graduate, and mentioning that my younger sister had joined the CIA.

I was vexed, but not surprised, that my parents should yet again harp on the length of time I was taking to get my degree; it is not as if they are paying more than a nominal part of my fees, but I am aware that they feel an undergraduate son of twenty-three to be a blot on their escutcheon.

However, I really did not wish to know that my sister had joined the CIA. There are times when

one prefers to live in ignorance of the igno-
minies of others, and this was one of those
times. I had always been aware that my sister
was mentally unbalanced, but I would have pre-
ferred to think the family had quietly mewed her
up in an asylum. I took my plate of eggplant, and
contemplated whether to chew up the letter for
dessert.

"What's wrong, Keith, you look like you just
swallowed a slug," said Dave, he and Myron
making a rare appearance in the dining room.

"It may be too vile to mention at dinner," I
said. Intentionally speaking with a mouth full of
eggplant, I said "My sister has joined the CIA."

"The **what?**" said Dave; evidently he had
heard me all too well.

"The CIA," I muttered.

"The **CIA?**" said Myron, looking up from his
plate for the first time and dropping slabs of
eggplant from his fork.

"You needn't broadcast it," I said. "I am ruined for life."

"Wait," said Dave, "who told you this? Is this some kind of threat?"

"Well, it wasn't exactly an anonymous note saying 'Leave town, your sister has joined the CIA,'" I said. "It was a letter from my mother."

"Here, let me see," said Dave, snatching the letter before I could stop him. He glanced at it and tossed it back. "There must be some mistake. They call the Culinary Institute of America the CIA, too, you know. She must've gone there. Nobody joins the other CIA anymore. They'd have to be crazy."

"Precisely," I said. "My sister."

"Well, have it your way. She's **your** sister. But I wouldn't believe it of **my** sister."

I ignored this and continued to eat. I had imagined that my family had already done everything in its power to annoy and embarrass me, but I had never dreamed that my sister would join the CIA. If the government did not already have files on me, it was bound to acquire them rapidly.

"Hey," said Tricia, appearing as if from nowhere, "look what I found downtown."

Setting down her tray and pulling out a chair, she displayed a pair of black fingerless lace gloves.

"Very interesting," I replied, inspecting them. Apparently the purchase of these bizarre little items had dispelled her gloom at reporting Gilbert and Lainey to the police; I wished the CIA could be disposed of so easily.

"And," she went on, "I'm going to dye my hair black."

Dave and Myron looked up in mutual surprise.

"Black?" said Dave. Tricia's natural hair color is a light brown. "Halloween's a little far in the future, isn't it?"

"I'm going to look just like Siouxsie Sioux," she replied blissfully, and I averted my eyes at this thought. I hoped that the rest of the Gang of Four was not planning on doing anything so ridiculous. As a diversionary tactic, I changed the subject.

"I was thinking of interviewing Dawnya Rankin again tonight. You seemed to put her a little more at ease last time; do you want to come along again?"

Tricia threw up her lace-covered hands. "That poor girl!" she exclaimed.

"Who's Dawnya Rankin?" inquired Dave; Myron arose to fetch another helping of eggplant.

Tricia and I explained who Dawnya Rankin was, and her place in our investigation of Richard Gurney's murder. Then Tricia said "But Keith, I don't know if I want to talk to any more people about it tonight. Especially Dawnya Rankin. That poor girl ..."

I reminded her that we ought to speak to "that poor girl" again in light of her newly revealed relationship with Gurney.

"I suppose," said Tricia dubiously, "but I have a lot of drawing to do, and I was going to get Pauline to help me dye my hair."

That decided me. Faced with the imminent prospect of Tricia dyeing her hair black, I exerted my most persuasive powers to assure her that if we spoke to Dawnya right after supper, she would have plenty of time to do her drawings, and even to read her anthropology assignment.

Perhaps distracted by the mention of her anthropology class, she agreed to join me. "After all," she said, "the poor girl might not even be there."

Myron and Dave then induced me to express a willingness to play Euchre later in the evening, and I felt that between the playing of Euchre and the further questioning of Dawnya Rankin, I would have sufficient matter to keep my thoughts from the CIA.

Dawnya, somewhat to our surprise, answered the door promptly upon our knock. The reason immediately became clear: Nila was not there to intercept her visitors.

"Can we talk to you again?" said Tricia kindly.

Dawnya nodded listlessly, and allowed us in. Her appearance was almost identical to before, except that the orange surfer-and-sunset T-shirt had been exchanged for a blue one stating that someone in Chicago loved her. I wondered briefly who this might be, but decided it was probably a relative.

I also wondered what had prompted Richard Gurney to interest himself in her; granted, she might prove attractive if she were ever to exhibit a trace of animation, but she seemed so unredeemably droopy that I felt this rather improbable. Was it her apparently passive nature that had caught his eye—her look of a woman unlikely to resist his advances?

"We understand," I said as politely as possible, "that you slept with Richard Gurney after one of his sherry parties."

Dawnya nodded, and it occurred to me that if a stranger had asked **me** about my recent sexual history, I would at least have demanded to know why I should tell them about it. However, that was another matter.

"Were you having an affair, or was it just a one-time thing?"

Dawnya looked even more miserable at this, but I refused to let it bother me, and after a moment she indicated that she had only slept with him the once.

"How did you feel about him?" said Tricia.

Dawnya appeared to consider this at great length, and stared out the window as though seeking advice from the clouds and vegetation outside. "I don't know," she replied eventually.

"Well, did you like him?" said Tricia.

This question was evidently no easier than its predecessor, and received the same answer.

Tricia and I were momentarily stumped. How were we to learn anything from a woman who professed not to know how she felt about Richard Gurney, or even if she had liked him? I decided to eschew delicacy.

"Well, how did you feel about finding him dead?" I asked.

But Dawnya only dissolved into tears at this.

26

"Keith, that was really mean of you!" exclaimed Tricia afterwards. "You made the poor girl cry all over again!"

There was no convincing her that Dawnya Rankin would have cried at some point no matter what I said; Tricia had made up her mind that I was cruel and inhuman. To make matters worse, she immediately stomped off to enlist Pauline in the hair-dyeing scheme.

Before I could sink too deeply into despair at the combined menace of my sister embracing the CIA and Tricia imitating Siouxsie Sioux, Dave and Myron arrived and Malcolm consented to join us for a few games of Euchre. Consequently, we retired to the lounge—our own lounge, not the lounge in which Lainey and Gilbert had found the ill-fated preceptor—and proceeded to deal the cards.

As Malcolm had spent the entire day biking, and Dave and Myron had not been by much all week, they indicated a desire to be briefed on the day's events.

However, they did not insist on extreme detail or exhaustive analysis—though they were entertained by my description of Pauline's conversation with Lainey and Gilbert—and before long we had returned to our usual, less talkative, manner of play. And this suited me well enough, as a number of vague ideas were inchoately circulating in my mind, none of them yet clear or comprehensible, yet all of them nagging at me in their inarticulate way. I did not know quite what any of them were trying to say; in fact, the sensation was much like that which occasionally afflicts me when I have read extensively on a given topic and am eager but not yet able to begin writing my paper. When under a tight deadline, this is infuriating; otherwise, I have come to accept it as a sign of what could be termed mental digestion. Information has been taken, but not yet fully absorbed.

Since this feeling generally presages a successful paper, I was more pleased than discomfited; after all, the game of Euchre, which occupies part but not all of the mind, ought to be an ideal accompaniment to this sort of half-conscious churning. I could think about my cards, and listen to Myron talk about his lab, and reply intelligently to Dave's talk of Asterix comics. I could—in passing—wonder what had possessed my sister to join the CIA, and whether Tricia's hair would really end up black. So long as I did not allow myself to think too hard about anything in particular, I might be able to speed up this restless and temporarily frustrating process, and emerge with a useful (or even brilliant) synthesis.

To be sure, none of this came to pass in exactly the convenient manner I had hoped.

After three or four games, we were interrupted by the advent of Carolyn, who had left rehearsal much in advance of Holly. She did not do more than poke her nose into the lounge, as she has never shown any interest in our card games, but her arrival abruptly changed the topic. As soon as she had refused our invitation to join and had safely retreated from the lounge, Myron voiced the plaint that she ignored him.

As this was unquestionably true, yet not a thing we felt we could in any charity explain to him, there was a moment of silence. Then Dave, who gets along well enough with Carolyn, said "Well, you know she doesn't play Euchre."

"She did once," said Myron, in the apparent belief that Carolyn's having once consented to a game was of some deep significance. In fact, she had totally failed to grasp anything about the game beyond the elementary fact that certain cards were more desirable than others; she had undergone the entire exercise with an expression of complete mystification, and had departed as soon as possible with the excuse of urgent study. This had been despite Dave's patient efforts to explain the rules, and his ongoing advice as to what to do with her cards.

"Doesn't she like me?" Myron continued.

I was tempted to ask why she **should** like him, but I suspected that, rather than placating him, this might set him off.

"Carolyn doesn't know you as well as we do," I said. "She doesn't play Euchre, she doesn't read science fiction, and she doesn't understand anything else you do either. She probably feels that the two of you have little in common."

Myron shifted in his appalling double-knits.

"Carolyn can be difficult at times," conceded Dave.

"Carolyn is **always** difficult," said Evan as he entered the room. "She is still worth knowing, of course." He sat down on the couch to observe the game. "Has she done something unusually stupid?"

Something in my brain seemed to fall into place, though I could not have said yet what it was.

"Not that I know of," I said. "We were speaking generally."

"Well, in general Carolyn strikes me as being incapable of making up her mind about life," said Evan. "She pursues a major in a less than academic field, she wastes a great deal of time reading medieval French poetry, and she spends the rest of her time thinking about sex."

The rest of us looked at him in some surprise.

"Where do you get that idea?" said Dave, not specifying whether he referred to life, sex, or both.

"And what's wrong with being a Theater major and reading medieval French poetry?"

"I think Carolyn has a perfectly good grasp on life," said Malcolm. "She doesn't seem to do any worse than any of the rest of us."

"That's a matter of opinion," said Evan; "besides, it doesn't matter what some people do. Carolyn should at least be ..."

There was a sound of some heavy object meeting masonry.

"What was **that?**" said Dave, turning.

The sound was repeated. There was no question in my mind but that Carolyn had heard some portion of our conversation and was now venting her annoyance on inanimate objects.

I was not certain what to do. Although we had ceased our discussion of Carolyn and continued our game of Euchre, we had not played for very much longer. After finishing the game in question, I had excused myself and gone to my room; it had then occurred to me to go back into the hallway, where I first heard Tricia exclaiming "How much longer now, Pauline?" and then, at Carolyn's door, an ominous silence.

Past experience has shown that in times of stress Carolyn is apt either to play loud music (it is true she also does this when happy or attempting to increase her typing speed), or to dispense with music altogether. The occasional flight of heavy objects was generally associated with a lack of music, but it was also possible that she had gone out.

I considered knocking, but, unsure what kind of wrath I might encounter, opted for a bath instead. I returned to my room, changed into my robe, and betook myself to the bathroom to fill the tub and take my towel and soap from their cubicle.

The bathtub in our Hall resides in solitary splendor in a small room separated from the main bathroom by two walls and a curtain; to the best of my knowledge, I am the only person to use it, as everyone else prefers the shower. Therefore, it is possible to soak in the tub for an hour or more without causing anyone the slightest inconvenience; thus, I returned to my room for a book.

I am aware that there are those who will persist in arguing that it is not possible to read in the tub without getting one's book wet: to them I reply only that they are frivolous shower-bathers who have never bothered to learn the art of reading in a bathtub.

The tub full and its water temperature perfected, I cast aside my robe and with my book in hand sank gratefully into the depths, where I remained for an unknown period of time, or at least until the cooling water and increasing chapter numbers alerted me to the passage of considerable time. Then, my willingness to face the world renewed, I emerged and dried myself. I entertained and dismissed the notion of shaving; put my bookmark in the appropriate place; and, putting on my robe and tying the belt, pulled open the curtain only to find Carolyn washing her face at the sink.

She seemed to be making a thorough job of it, with much splashing. I put away my soap and towel and said "How was rehearsal?"

"Horrible."

Her nose sounded suspiciously congested. I said "Is Holly back yet?"

"No."

I said "You sound rather upset."

Carolyn turned off the water and turned to face me with her towel in her face. When she removed the towel, I could see that her eyes were still red. "I **am** upset. So what?"

"I just wondered."

"So I'm upset. Who cares? I have a shitty rehearsal of a stupid play with uncooperative actors that I should never have agreed to work on; I have poems to read and a scene to rehearse and people being killed practically next door, and Evan Reid goes around telling people I spend all my time thinking about sex."

"Hmm," I said.

"I'm going to kill him! Where does he get this idea that I'm obsessed with sex?"

I did not point out that he might have gotten it from her tendency, shared with Holly, to bring the topic into half their conversations; after all, neither I nor anyone else take this as more than an indication of their interest in it. Interest does not equal obsession.

"It's not fair. He goes around telling everyone I'm a sex maniac and don't belong in a university, when I spend all my time working and haven't had sex with anybody in about a million years."

The image came to me of a paleolithic Carolyn writhing passionately somewhere in the dust of

Olduvai Gorge. "Well, you shouldn't pay any attention to him. Nobody else does."

"They do too. Everybody's always listening to Evan's stupid speeches."

I sighed. "Just because people listen to him doesn't mean they take everything he says seriously. People aren't going to put greater weight on some ill-considered remark of Evan's than on their own knowledge of you."

"Well, I'm still going to kill him," said Carolyn. Unlike some people, her comments did not seem to be chastened by the happenstance of murder, and I was reminded that this was the first time I had had a chance to speak with Carolyn alone since the night we had discovered the body. I was still curious just what the Gang of Four was up to, and why the other three had prevented me from speaking with Carolyn after the murder.

"I realize Evan can be annoying," I said, "but really, the main result of killing him would be that everyone would assume you'd killed Richard Gurney as well."

"If I'd already killed Evan," said Carolyn, almost but not quite smiling, "what difference would it make if people thought I'd killed Richard Gurney?" Her face lost all possibility of a smile. "Besides, what if I **had** killed him?"

I looked at her carefully. Her eyes were still red and puffy, and as she stood there in her black fatigues, oversized painting shirt, and peacock-blue Chinese shoes, she seemed altogether incapable of killing anyone. "Carolyn," I said, "why do you keep insisting that you might have killed Richard Gurney? I don't know why you would, but if by some strange chance you did, why don't you say so? If you're going to go around killing people, you should either shut up about it or confess; there's no other rational alternative."

Carolyn took a deep breath and then let it out with some exasperation. "Do you really think I killed Richard Gurney?" she demanded.

"Of course not."

"Well, of course I didn't!" she returned, staring up at me as if I had lost my mind. "I'm not about to kill anybody, even if I **am** going to kill Evan."

I ignored her concluding paradox. "Well, then why do you keep trying to get people to think that you **did** kill Gurney, and why do Holly and Tricia and Pauline keep behaving as though you have to be protected and prevented from incriminating yourself and God only knows what else? They seem to have set up an entirely separate investigation which only sometimes leaks any information to anyone else. What on earth is going on?"

Carolyn turned her head and gazed fixedly in the direction of the toilets. "It was one of those stupid things. I slept with him last year."

27

I was considerably taken aback by this confession. Carolyn sleep with Richard Gurney? It seemed unimaginable. And yet of course it fit.

"I don't know why I did it," said Carolyn. "As soon as I got in bed with him, I knew it was a mistake. I knew even before ... Oh, I don't know when I knew, I just **knew.**"

"Well then why," I could not refrain from asking, "didn't you just tell him to forget the whole thing and leave?"

Carolyn thought about this. "Well, of course I should have, but that wouldn't've been fair, I'd already given him the idea I would. It didn't seem right to back out at that point."

For an educated and supposedly liberated woman, this seemed a strangely archaic and self-destructive attitude. Still, I have noticed that even the most determined feminists are far better at advising their friends than they are at making any personal use of their insights. And though I sometimes find this sad, ridiculous, or frustrating, I am aware that this is only human. We are taught to think of other people's feelings, and no doubt this admirable but inappropriate precept had governed Carolyn's behavior when she found herself in Richard Gurney's bed.

"It's really stupid," Carolyn was saying now, "the way all those sex education books talk about how it's up to the woman to say no because men have no self-control. Men have plenty of self-control! Every man I've ever wanted to sleep with has said no!" She took a breath and plunged on. "So when everyone you **want** says no, it's harder to refuse the ones you **don't** want. The whole thing is fucked."

Having said this, she stared fixedly at the floor, hunching her shoulders as though the bathroom had taken on an arctic chill.

"You really shouldn't take this so seriously," I said. "Not to belittle its importance, but ..."

"How can I **not** take it seriously?" she exclaimed, momentarily abandoning her inspection of the bathroom tile.

"Well, things change as you get older." I shrugged. "Someone'll say yes. In any case, you can't let it interfere with your life."

This, predictably, did not satisfy her. I had not expected that it would.

"In any case," I went on, "I'm rather curious about Holly and the others. Do they think you killed Gurney, or what?"

"Of course not. They just don't think anybody should find out I slept with him, which is fine with me. God, I wish I'd never heard of him."

"But they seem to be conducting a whole separate investigation. When I talked to Theo, he said Holly had already been on his case, and she hasn't said a word about it to me."

"Well, Holly figures that if we find out who really killed Gurney, nobody has to know that I slept with him."

"Including, I suppose, the rest of the Hall?"

"Well, yes ... I mean, what if Evan heard about it? He'd never let me forget it."

I gave up. The rest of the Gang of Four was going to hear from me in the morning.

Sunday began much as had Saturday. Again, as I lay cozily in bed wondering whether to open my eyes yet, I heard the faint strains of Carolyn's stereo; this time she was playing Vivaldi. Relieved that this time she was not inclined towards songs of death and mayhem, and assuming from this that she had not only survived the night but regained a measure of equanimity, I did not bother to open my eyes until she had worked her way through both sides of the record and gone on to Stravinsky's **Rite of Spring.**

Not feeling that the **Rite of Spring,** despite its innocuous title, was conducive to further repose, I now bestirred myself to slide out of bed and dress. A look in the mirror suggested that I might also take the trouble to shave, but I could not summon any enthusiasm for that yet. I looked at my Tintin clock.

It wanted half an hour till brunch.

I thought about study. Indeed, I thought about Voltaire and the Enlightenment. The thought of Voltaire and the Enlightenment led me to the further thought that Voltaire was a crafty sort who would undoubtedly have been able to figure out not only that Carolyn had slept with Richard Gurney (after all, I had a feeling that this was one of the things that had been stirring about in the back of my mind), but who would have solved the entire mess by this time and offered the results of his enlightenment to the police.

Or, thinking in terms of European diplomatic history, I was equally certain that such scheming fellows as Talleyrand and Bismarck, with their networks of spies and informers, would rapidly have acquired all the information they needed and would have immediately recognized the pattern therein, allowing them to nab the malefactor and deal summarily with him—perhaps, I allowed myself to digress, by depriving him of valuable industrial territories or a strategic military corridor.

However, at the notion of a murderer deprived not of liberty but of industrial territories, I put a stop to my imaginings. This tendency to create impossible scenarios might amuse me, but it was of no use in either the study of history or the solving of crimes. It was as inutile as Tricia's cufflinks or Carolyn's psychopaths, or the idea that someone had killed Gurney in a fit of revulsion at his unwanted advances.

I realized that that had been Carolyn's suggestion, too. More sex. **Was** Carolyn obsessed with sex? Why would anyone kill someone for such a ridiculous reason—I had heard nothing to indicate that Gurney was a rapist, merely that he seemed unselective and either favored or was stuck with one-night stands. Well, it was Carolyn's idea, along with the Russians and the CIA (heaven forbid!) and gang warfare.

I had the feeling that something was indeed forming in some dark and murky region of my mind, but although it embarrasses me now to confess it, I had not yet recognized the answer.

And perhaps if I had not looked at the clock again and seen that it was time for brunch—no, I was too eager to confront Holly about her inquiries. I picked up meal card and keys, and was off down the stairs.

Holly had already staked out her place at the table, and was sitting alone with a bowl of cereal, her morning coffee, and the ever-present datebook. I was surprised that she had not stopped to get Carolyn on her way down, since if they are both in the dorm they will generally come to meals together, but before I could inquire about this she jabbed her pencil at the datebook and said "Actors!"

"Actors?" I repeated. "What of them? Isn't your show about to open?"

"Yes," said Holly, "and that's precisely it." She gave her shoulders an irritable shake like that of a sprinkled cat. "Actors have **no** appreciation of tech. And neither do directors. They all think it's going to magically appear at dress rehearsal, without any time, trouble, money, or help."

I gave a sympathetic nod, although I had heard this complaint innumerable times before both from her and from Carolyn.

"Do you realize what they went and did yesterday?" she went on; I indicated a willingness to listen. "The lighting people were scheduled to hang and focus all day and the pieces of the set were supposed to get nailed into place last night while the lights were finishing, and when Carolyn and I got there to look things over last night, we found out that **without telling us**" (evidently this was a mortal sin in and of itself) "**without telling us,** these so-called actors and their so-called director had insisted on having an extra rehearsal around the hanging and focusing."

Even with my limited experience of theater, I recognized that this was a move of great folly. "Why didn't they rehearse somewhere else?" I asked. "There are plenty of drama studios, aren't there?"

Holly was icy. "They hadn't bothered to book one because they had the theater already."

"But isn't it your job to book the space?"

"Of course it is, but they have to tell me what they want. So there they were, getting in the way of the lights and everybody arguing because you can't hang lights during a rehearsal and you can't rehearse when people are hanging lights, and both sides were convinced that they were right, only of course the lighting designer, who actually **was** right, couldn't throw out the director."

I wondered whether anyone had thrown anything else; it sounded like that kind of situation.

"And when Carolyn and I got there, it was a total madhouse and nobody was getting anything done at all, and the assistant director asked Carolyn who she was and whether she was part of the show, which shows what kind of a wandering idiot the AD is, so Carolyn said that if nobody wanted her to work on this show she was leaving right then, because she had better things to do and it was the most asinine show she'd ever worked on." Holly took a breath. "So Carolyn **left,** and I was stuck there all night by myself dealing with these **maniacs.**"

"I see." It did not sound as though Holly appreciated Carolyn's departure, even if she thought it justified. "Now I see why Carolyn was so upset last night."

"Why, what'd she **do?**" demanded Holly.

"She was just upset," I said, avoiding the details, "and I hadn't realized that the rehearsal had gone so badly."

"Badly!" said Holly. "It was nonexistent! It was insane! So help me, it was the most unprofessional bunch of posturing nitwits I've ever seen!"

Her lower lip began to tremble, and I suspected that without the coffee she was now hastily fortifying herself with, and without the moral support of Carolyn, she had probably lost her composure in front of the entire cast and crew. It had happened at least once before, though she did not like to talk about it.

I turned the conversation back to Carolyn. "Carolyn happened to mention," I said, "that you and the rest of the Gang of Four had taken on your own separate murder investigation in order to prevent anyone from finding out that she had slept with Richard Gurney."

Holly slammed down her coffee and looked up at me, dumfounded. "What the hell did she tell you that for?"

28

"Well, really, Holly," I said, "why shouldn't she?"

Holly stared as if the sight of me had caused her to lose all ability to speak.

"It is not," I went on, "as though I reviled her for immorality, threatened her for withholding information, or even chastised her for being foolish. Furthermore, it is not as though I have any intention of mentioning her past mistakes to anyone who is not already familiar with them, because I really do not see the importance of them."

"But ..." began Holly uselessly; she could not seem, however, to finish her sentence.

"If Carolyn slept with Gurney last year and regretted it at the time, then why would she want to kill him now? I admit that anything is possible, but I'm convinced that Carolyn had nothing at all to do with the murder, and that all you have done is bring attention to something she would rather forget."

"That's all very well for **you** to say, Keith," said Holly, finding her voice, "but what if someone like Evan had found out—or have you already gone and told him? He'd never let her have any peace, he'd always be making snide remarks about her taste in men or something."

"It's hard to say how Evan might take it," I noted; "he might make life difficult for her or then again he might decide to be charitable and never mention it."

Holly did not look as though she thought the latter to be possible; she rolled her eyes and tilted her head most skeptically.

"But since Carolyn would never tell him, and since none of the rest of us are likely to mention it to anyone ... The point is that there was no reason for anyone to find out anything about it, so why draw attention to it with all this secrecy and rigmarole? It was obvious from the beginning that something was going on."

"Keith," said Holly, "you are just **nosy.** If you weren't so damn **nosy** you would never have noticed a thing."

"You mean," I returned, "that if I had been lacking a normal ability to observe my surroundings, I might not have noticed anything." I took a bite from my English muffin, now long cold. "**But,** since I do **not** lack this ordinary and important faculty, it was glaringly apparent that you were up to something, and that you yourself were nosing into things like a ..." I recalled Theo's comparison, "... like a bloodhound."

"**Well,**" said Holly with great firmness, in a tone I suspected her of using to keep rebellious actors in line, "there's no need to get snippy."

Snippy was exactly the term I would have applied to her own remarks, had I but thought of it first. "I am not being **snippy,** I am pointing out that it was foolish and unproductive of you to set off on an entirely separate investigation—not to mention that it was altogether uncomradely."

"Uncomradely!" came the voice of Carolyn from somewhere behind me. "What are you talking about, Communist Russia?"

I turned, and saw not only Carolyn, but Tricia as well: Tricia's hair was now an uneven hue of black, which she had emphasized with a great deal of matching eye makeup, and echoed with the fingerless black lace gloves. Her denim jacket was, as usual, festooned with Talking Heads pins and a picture of Johnny Rotten. It seemed a remarkable ensemble for Sunday brunch, especially on a person also devoted to Petula Clark, **Mary Poppins**, and various British folk singers; and Holly gazed at it with dubious wonder and some distaste. Not far behind Tricia was Pauline, also with new hair, excessive eye makeup, and—less startling in that she had worn similar items before—a neon orange T-shirt over a green leather miniskirt, with so enormous a peace sign around her neck that I anticipated it would soon raise a bruise. Carolyn, in contrast, was dressed much as usual in her black fatigues, blue Chinese shoes, and a different painting shirt than she had worn the night before.

"Sit down," I said. "We are actually discussing not Communist Russia—or, as they prefer to be called, the Soviet Union—but your independent investigations into Richard Gurney's death."

"Oh!" said Tricia, glancing at Holly and Carolyn. Holly had the look of a pot that would like to boil over but cannot quite bring itself to do so. Carolyn's expression was no more remarkable than her apparel.

"I am aware," I went on, "of the reason behind these investigations, and I have no interest in it beyond that of personal concern for Carolyn. However, I am **quite** interested in whatever you might have discovered and what until now you have so annoyingly failed to mention to the rest of us."

The Gang of Four looked at one another as though this might prove of some assistance in deciding what to say.

"Well," said Tricia, "we interviewed a lot of people."

This was excellent, since I felt I had not managed to interview nearly enough; I had not even run across anyone who claimed to have seen Gurney on the day he was murdered. "Who did you interview?" I asked.

"Oh ... Theo Roth, all the preceptors, Gurney's RAs, everyone on Liz's Hall ... Who else?"

"Who else?" Holly consulted her book. "The college secretaries, both proctors, Gurney's old flame Dorie who left school, his thesis advisor ... Need I go on?"

Need she go on? My mind was in disorder at the thought of so many interviews. How had they accomplished this by any means other than that of sending out a general questionnaire?

"I am amazed," I said, "amazed and stunned."

"When things are properly organized," said Holly primly, "it is not difficult to get a lot done."

I gathered that she did not think most things in this world, including my time, were properly organized, but since I knew perfectly well that Holly herself is well organized only about fifty percent of the time, I did not take this as a slight.

"Well," I said, "I would very much like to hear your results, not to mention your stratagem for interrogating Gurney's thesis advisor."

"The thesis advisor was easy," said Carolyn.

I looked at her in surprise. "Indeed?" It would be particularly surprising if Carolyn herself had spoken with the advisor.

"Piece of cake," she said. She then admitted that she had not actually anticipated anything of the sort. "I didn't think I'd get anywhere on it, but I went to the Department and asked who his advisor was, with the general idea that if one of us knew the person ... I was expecting it might be one of Liz's professors, but it turned out to be someone I'd had a class with, so since he'd been pretty impressed with my work, I wandered down to his office and nabbed him."

"What did he say?"

"Well, we had quite a nice conversation about this and that, but the Richard Gurney part of it wasn't especially enlightening. He said that Gurney was supposed to be doing a thesis on Kurt Vonnegut, but that he hadn't seen much of said thesis and that he didn't think he could write for shit."

"Gurney or Vonnegut?" I asked.

"Gurney, of course. I couldn't tell what he thought of Vonnegut, but apparently the paper was supposed to deal with sociological aspects of Vonnegut's thought, and I don't think he thought much of that. Or maybe it was just Gurney's dreary prose that didn't impress him."

I said "I am sure that this is of no real importance, but curiosity demands that I ask whether this nameless professor actually described Gurney's style as dreary and whether he actually stated Gurney couldn't write for shit."

Carolyn lowered her eyes delicately. "I think he actually said something to the effect of Gurney's writing being quite unmemorable and below the standards set by some of his undergraduate students."

"Meaning you," said Holly.

"That was my impression," said Carolyn, "since he went on to say that he was much more interested in my academic progress than in who killed Richard Gurney, and that he hoped I would take one of his upper-division courses next quarter."

"Oh," I said. "So you were not able to find out anything about Gurney's life or connections from this professor."

"Not really," said Carolyn. "He said that he had just asked Gurney to submit a longer reading list for the thesis, but that was purely because the original reading list was so inadequate."

"I see," I said. As I had thought, Gurney was of limited ability, at least in his chosen field. Perhaps English had been the "easy" major at his previous school, as Psychology seemed to be in others. But as Voltaire so acutely remarked, in order to get anywhere in this world, it is not enough to be stupid, one must also have good manners.

"If you really want a run-down on all the inter-views, you'd better look at our notes," said Holly. "Otherwise we'll be here all afternoon, and **some** of us"—she looked at Carolyn as if expecting a response—"have to be at the theater at one."

It was of course nowhere near one yet, but on the other hand it was not so far from it that a detailed accounting of all the people mentioned could be accomplished in the interim.

"Are your notes readable?" I inquired.

"Readable?" said Pauline.

"Readable?" said Holly; "they're typed!"

"You **typed** them?" I was again astounded; who would have imagined it?

"Carolyn typed them," said Tricia. "She hates to interview people and she types fast, so we made her type 'em."

"Come on, if you want to see them we'd better go up now," said Holly.

Up in Carolyn's room—or, more accurately, in Carolyn's doorway, as her floor is covered with stacks of books and papers that her desk and shelves somehow cannot accommodate—we waited as she sifted her way through the desk-stack.

But despite the daunting size and varicolored nature of the stack (in addition to circulars, old newspapers, a book on Guillaume de Machaut, and an empty bag of hamster litter, we were shown an issue of **Theater Crafts** that allegedly showed Carolyn fiberglassing a six-foot maple leaf), she located the notes in remarkably short order.

"These're the ones," she said, riffling rapidly through them and changing the order of a few.

"Thanks," I said, glancing through them myself. "Do you mind if I keep these for the day?"

"Just don't lose them," said Holly.

The idea that I would somehow lose valuable documents in the course of a quiet afternoon at home was rather insulting, but I refrained from comment in the interest of peace. Instead, I said "They shall not leave my room," which was a mistake since I immediately realized that it would be far more pleasant to read them in the coffee shop or the Quad.

"All right, then get thee to thy room," said Carolyn, laughing. "You won't be allowed out until you've read them **and** solved the murder."

At that, they all laughed, and exited severally.

29

Ensconced in my room with notes, paper, and pen, I began to read. And although I suppose I should have expected it, I was nonetheless surprised at the quality of Carolyn's prose. Instead of contenting herself with the likes of "Tricia: Dorie Bethel: zilch," she had filled in a gratifying number of details.

"Tricia obtained the phone number of the former Dorie Bethel," she had written, "formerly a student and formerly RG's lover but now married and a leading light of the Mormon church of Provo, Utah ..." (I imagined the former Dorie Bethel expounding on her new life of virtue over the long-distance line, undoubtedly at the expense of

Tricia's parents) "... from the College secretaries." I also wondered how readily Kathy and Linda normally gave out phone numbers, but read on.

"Dorie informed Tricia that—having returned to the bosom of her church and family and thereby having fulfilled God's will despite her year of error and rebellion at the godless university—she had married her high school sweetheart, produced two beautiful twins ..." (I wondered whether Dorie or Carolyn had committed the redundancy of the two twins; I decided it must be Dorie, and fell briefly to imagining the possibilities of three twins, two sets of twins, and twins of which one was beautiful and the other resembled Bela Lugosi) "... and that she was not now, and never had been, in communication with her former lover RG. She further stated that she would resume praying for him, and offered to pray for Tricia as well in the hope that Tricia would leave school and become a Mormon." Become a Mormon? "Tricia did not mention that she was perfectly content to remain a lapsed Episcopalian."

I had not realized either that Tricia had once been an Episcopalian or that one "lapsed" from any church but the Catholic; in any case, it appeared that the former Dorie Bethel had refused further comment on Richard Gurney.

Skimming the report of Holly's interrogation of the College secretaries, I learned that Kathy and Linda had referred to Gurney as "that twit who was always looking for twat," and that in their opinion Liz's rabbit had committed the murder but that they were confident the police would soon arrest Holly and me.

Theo Roth had told Holly of hiring Gurney in a dearth of applicants for the position, and that Gurney had done his undergraduate work at one of the state colleges but had worked in construction and as a shipping clerk for several years prior to venturing to get his MA. "Theo assured Holly that RG had been perfectly ordinary throughout his job interview, wearing ordinary clothes, speaking in an ordinary voice, and having ordinary references. Theo further assured Holly that RG was entirely lacking in any police record, and had no reputation as a pickpocket, kleptomaniac, drunk, drug dealer, exhibitionist, or child molester. Theo informed Holly that he did not keep track of RG's love life and that he had received no complaints of sexual harassment against RG; he informed Holly that if there were women who felt that they had been harassed or otherwise wronged by RG, they should have mentioned it to someone. Eventually Theo pointed out that he had work to do and that if Holly required further information she should ask Keith."

The reports of Gurney's fellow preceptors indicated a lack of desire to speak ill of the dead, with correspondingly little information, while the report of Relief Proctor Sally told me nothing I had

not already heard. Proctor Hank had commented that Gurney drank heavily at parties, but had
added mildly that so did we.

Gurney's RAs were somewhat more informative. JoAnne's remarks were essentially those I
had already heard, but I was unfamiliar with
Pam and Josh's contributions.

"Liz inquired as to what Pam, her RA, thought
of RG and was told that he was of no use to
anyone since if no one ever wanted to hang out
with him and he wasn't any good at dealing with
suicidal students and all he was going to do at
his sherry parties was seduce freshmen, then what
was the use of having him?" Carolyn added that
Liz had explained that "Pam's inclusion of suicidal students referred to the case of Wally, a strange
and withdrawn type who ate a bottle of pills one
day in Pam's absence and who upon being revived
by his roommate had nothing to say to either the

roommate or to RG but permitted the room-mate to dial 911."

I really did not see why Pam should hold this last incident against Gurney, but decided I would reserve judgement until I had read the notes about Wally.

"Pauline's questioning of RG's third RA, Josh, elicited the information that he didn't pay any attention to that fucking bozo unless it was a question of something like handing out disaster drill pamphlets. He stated that he had no quarrel with preceptors so long as they minded their own business, gave good parties, and didn't mess with his Hall and its very profitable San Pedro cactus industry. He claimed that RG had prevented his Hall from painting its walls black, and that RG's parties sucked, but that RG was always hanging around everyone else's sniffing out free booze. Josh admitted to having attended one of RG's sherry parties and to have told RG to lay off Zoe Vogel and quit acting like a dickhead."

I wondered whether the admonishment to quit acting like a dickhead was a fact or merely an embellishment; in any case it seemed that Gurney had not cared about the farm of hallucinogenic cacti so long as the walls surrounding it were not black, so, knowing Josh, I did not think he had committed the murder.

Having now made my way through all of the employees interviewed, I turned my attention to Liz's Hall and the testimony of the suicidal Wally.

"Liz's attempt to question Wally was made difficult by his profound lack of interest in the topic. He averred that he had not attended any of the sherry parties because he hated parties and didn't drink, and claimed to have first met RG on the occasion of his (own) suicide attempt. He stated that the sight of RG always reminded him of this attempt, and said that he always feels very depressed anyway. He then went on to talk at length about being depressed. Liz states that she can't stand Wally because he's creepy and his room smells like old socks."

So much for Wally. His roommate, John, had said only that Gurney had not been very useful in dealing with Wally, and that the sooner he (John) moved into a single room the happier he would be.

So I read on. Carolyn's accounts of Liz's conversations with Steve Madison, Nila and Dawnya, Jerry and Doug, and her other hall-mates amused me, but as they were not overwhelmingly informative, and proved to have no bearing on the case, I shall not include them. For as Voltaire has said, the secret of being a bore is to tell everything.

When I came to Renee and Zoe, however, I read more carefully; after all, Renee had reported the vagrant in the lounge.

"According to Tricia, Renee discovered the alleged vagrant (RG) because Zoe and Bronwen were arguing in her room when she returned from class, and she wanted a quiet place to study before going to dinner. She said that the body was lying facing the back of the couch, and that as far as she could see it was entirely covered by a blanket except for the back of the head. Renee said she did not look closely, but immediately went to tell the RA, Pam. However, Pam was not home, so when she saw later that the body was still there, she called in a report for Sally."

The main interest of this seemed to be that Renee had found the body, which I already knew; still, I felt it important to have this information in as much detail as possible.

"Tricia is of the opinion that Renee was unusually reticent, even evasive, during their conversation. Remembering that Renee had already known of the murder when we encountered her downtown, she asked how Renee heard about it, but Renee was vague and said she had heard about it somewhere around the Hall. Tricia was unable to get more specific details from her, and says that although Renee is somewhat reserved, it was weird that she was so reluctant to discuss the murder. Tricia says the whole conversation made her feel funny, and that she knows Renee isn't telling something."

I thought about this for a moment before going on to Zoe.

"Liz located Zoe only with great difficulty, as Zoe is practically never home anymore. Zoe struck Liz as being incredibly depressed, and explained that, dorm life having become intolerable, she is moving downtown to live with her friend Bronwen. She remarked that living downtown would remove the temptation to jump out of dorm room windows; Liz said that this was supposed to be a joke but that Zoe looked serious. When questioned about RG, Zoe said she had nothing to say. When questioned about RG's advances to her at the sherry party, Zoe stated that now that he was dead she had nothing to say about that either. When further questioned why his being dead should prevent her from discussing the sherry party, Zoe went to the window and said with considerable agitation that she had too many other things on her mind to be talking about RG and his damned sherry party. Liz apologized and withdrew."

I put down some notes and questions of my own, and stood up to stretch and tap Carolyn's papers back into line. But as I was turning them sideways on my desk and simultaneously turning over their contents in my mind, the back pages buckled rebelliously and slid out of my hands onto the floor behind the desk. Muttering the usual curses, I got down on hand and knee to find them lying next to the wall along with three paperclips, a favorite pen, and a dust ball of embarrassing proportions.

I also found the note that had been affixed to my door Friday night, which I had not yet read and which I had subsequently unaccountably forgotten.

I shall not torment the reader with long and drawn-out descriptions of my activities during the remainder of that day or the next, for although the latter part of Sunday was not a blank, and although I had a number of very important arrangements to make on Monday ...

Suffice it to say that the note on my door, while in itself containing no actual clues or information, proved the necessary catalyst to jog my sluggish brain. As if by magic or some trick of stagecraft, the roiling murk that had lately characterized my thoughts was replaced by clear and logical certainty. The identity of the killer, which should have been long since plain, was now obvious to me. Consequently, I required time to make my plans, and then to assure the assistance and silence of my confederates. On Monday morning I paid a visit to the Health Center; on Monday afternoon Mariah Sebastian dropped in to ask for information that I was unwilling yet to provide. On Monday evening, Evan and I attended Chong's class as usual, noted that which we had anticipated but hoped against, and went home. In my room, while Evan alerted the others, I prepared myself for confrontation.

As ready as I would ever be for one of the most unwelcome tasks of my life—yet one that I could not feel justified in leaving to the police—I went out of the Hall, past the stairs, past the trash closet, past Steve Madison's room and the lounge, and knocked on a familiar door.

"Who's there?" said an even more familiar voice.

"Keith," I said.

She opened the door and looked at me. And as she looked, her eyes widened and filled with tears.

"I wish it hadn't been you," she said, the tears spilling as she turned away and let me in.

30

We sat down on her bed; she had already surreptitiously wiped the tears during the few steps from the door. All along her side of the room were boxes and a curiously premature sense of vacancy, as if not only were her belongings packed but both she and they had already gone, leaving but an illusion in their place.

I shook off this unsettling feeling and looked at her.

"You can take off the damned neck brace," she said after a moment. "You know perfectly well I'm not going to kill you too."

"It was just a thought," I said, complying. "Not so much in terms of self-protection as with the notion of making things easier."

She looked away. "I'm not sure whether I'd prefer to believe that or not. After all, it's silly to go off to meet murderers without some form of protection."

"This is so," I agreed. "And as Voltaire once remarked, 'I am very fond of truth, but not at all of martyrdom.'"

She smiled a little at this. "That's right, you're taking Voltaire and the Enlightenment. Is it any good?"

"The topic is more interesting than the class. You should have taken it and livened things up."

"Not my field," she said. "I had other courses to get in. Besides, I haven't been very lively of late. It'll be a wonder if I pass anything, not that it matters anymore. When did you figure out it was me?"

"When I read your note."

She stared at me, and said "You mean you've known all weekend? Is that why you didn't come by until now?" Then she said, "Wait a second, what did I put in the note? There wasn't anything in the note—how could there have been?"

"It wasn't the note per se, it was the timing," I said. "I didn't actually read it until yesterday."

"Why; what was yesterday?"

"Nothing. Evidently it was time for me to guess, and when I read the note I knew. I can't explain how; that's just how my mind works sometimes."

She looked altogether skeptical, and with some cause. "I hope that's not how you plan to defend your Ph.D. dissertation."

"Hardly," I said. "Quite apart from the fact that my dissertation remains some years in the future, there is a great difference between the defense of it and the research and writing of it. And at the moment, the important thing is not how I arrived at my conclusions, but that they are correct.”

“Well,” she said, taking a deep breath, “if you have no evidence to support your conclusions, I can always deny that I ever admitted anything to you.”

“You could do that despite my evidence; but I don’t think that you will. Why don’t you just tell me the whole thing and be done with it?”

“Keith, I will never be done with it. Telling you will only mark the beginning of a different part of it. God dammit, why did **you** have to be the one? Why couldn’t it have been some goddamn policeman? Why did any of my friends have to be involved with this?”

I was about to say that I had not felt it right to simply call the police and ask them to haul her unceremoniously away—which I realized was precisely the feeling that had motivated Pauline to insist that she speak with Gilbert and Lainey—but

I stopped myself. "Who else is mixed up in this? Obviously someone helped you drag the body into the lounge."

She looked away again, and I could see more tears gathering against her will, tears that did not fall, but remained glistening in place. "Bronwen," she said. "Bronwen helped me."

"Bronwen," I repeated. Of course, I had already surmised this, but one's assumptions do not invariably prove correct. After all, it might rather have been Lina Troyer. "How did Bronwen end up helping you?"

"Because," said Zoe. "Because she was there."

I was taken aback. "What, she was there when you killed him?"

"No," said Zoe, shutting her eyes very tight. "If Bronwen had been there I wouldn't have killed him. If she had been there earlier it would never have happened at all. She just ... came in too late."

"But why did you kill him? The sherry party was just a stupid incident. The man was an asshole. Surely you could have just ignored him. What was he doing in your room?"

Her eyes still closed, Zoe rocked forward till her head lay between her knees. "He came upstairs," she said indistinctly, "and started telling me that it was too bad a nice girl like me had to think I was gay. He said that once I had made it with a guy like him, I'd know what I'd been missing."

She took a breath. "I told him I already knew what I was missing and I knew it wasn't anything I wanted, especially if it came with **his** attribut- es. Goddammit, his fucking **arrogance,** it isn't as though I hate men but men like him make me want to hate all of you, goddamn insensitive pricks who think they're the answer to everything in the goddamn fucking world—how dare he talk to me like that!" Her voice quieted again. "But I've heard all that before from other idiots including some well-meaning ones—"

I wondered if I had ever misguidedly suggested that she try sleeping with a man; I did not think so, but the possibility existed.

"—so it wasn't that, it was when he started hinting that Lina wouldn't get tenure if everybody knew she was having an affair with a student. Fucking bastard! The fucking blackmailer! 'Come on, Zoe, gimme some, why don'tcha?' I could kill him again right now!"

She sat up straight and looked intently at me, her fists rigid at her sides. "The fucking bastard! Goddammit, it's not like I meant to kill him, but I did mean it. I meant it when I did it. I did mean it, and what the hell am I going to do?"

"Does Lina know?" I asked.

Zoe seemed to collapse again inside. "No, no, no," she said, "how could I tell her a thing like that? How could I possibly tell her? My God, how could she live with the idea that I had killed somebody on her account?"

I shrugged. "Some people don't seem to have any trouble living with that kind of thing. Some people would probably think you had passed a test of devotion."

"Yes, and spend the rest of their lives wondering if I was going to kill them next."

"Probably," I agreed.

"Well, obviously I couldn't tell Lina," said Zoe. "Obviously I can't ever see her again."

"What are you talking about?" This seemed an extreme decision, even in an extreme situation.

"How can I possibly see her? I've **killed** somebody! The best I can do is to let her go on with her life without me."

"Zoe, that's ridiculous. You have to at least tell her what the situation is."

"I don't have to tell her anything," said Zoe. "Up to now Bronwen's been the only person who knew. When I told her I was thinking about turning myself in, she said there was no point in giving in to the patriarchy, and she's probably right."

"Telling Lina has nothing to do with the patriarchy!" I said, annoyed in spite of myself. After all, if someone were dropping me, I would want to know whether they had committed murder on my behalf or were merely sick of me, and I do not think myself alone in that attitude.

"No, but it all comes to the same thing," said Zoe wearily. "Whether I tell Lina, the police, or nobody, I still have to live with it."

"Naturally."

"Whether I make a radical lesbian choice and figure I've struck a necessary blow as my contribution to the struggle ..."

I could not find this an appealing idea.

"... or whether I make a traditional choice and figure I've done wrong no matter who I killed ..."

This seemed more rational to me, but perhaps I was unduly influenced by my gender.

"... I still have to live with it." Zoe looked at me again. "Oh God, Keith, what the hell am I going to do?"

She looked so forlorn that it was immaterial that she was gay and had killed Richard Gurney only a week before; I put my arms around her and she permitted herself to weep copiously into my shirt. After all, we were still friends.

She did not weep very long, however; soon there was a knock on the door and a tall woman who looked perfectly capable of moving any number of bodies came in, saying "Okay, Zoe, the truck's parked downstairs." She broke off upon seeing us and said "What the fuck is going on?"

I gathered that she was not pleased to see me, and I was tempted to be facetious and say that really, things were not as they seemed, but I restrained myself. Zoe disentangled herself from my shirt, and said "Keith knows."

"Well goddammit," said the other woman, evidently Bronwen Bay Laurel. She closed the door with considerable vehemence, without, however, actually slamming it. "What the hell business is it of his?"

I was beginning to wonder this myself. Maybe it was all for the best that Gurney was dead; perhaps despite all appearances we were living in the best of all possible worlds. On the other hand, I had apprised Evan and a number of other people of my plans, and no matter how great my fondness for Zoe nor how high my regard for her abilities, I was still of the general belief that one should not go about killing people.

"What difference does it make whether it's any business of his?" said Zoe. "He knows I did it."

"Well," said Bronwen, turning to me, "what do you propose to do about it?"

"I think Zoe should tell the police."

For an instant I thought Bronwen was going to spit in my face; to my relief, she did not. "You know, you're a real idiot," she said, "a real self-righteous idiot. What good is that going to do? All it'll do is ruin Zoe's life. It won't bring back that bastard Gurney, as if anyone wanted him back anyway. You want to throw Zoe into the jaws of the System."

Perhaps I **was** being a self-righteous idiot, but still. "I agree that one shouldn't give in to the System unnecessarily ..."

Bronwen looked at me as if I were a mentally defective male chauvinist lackey of the State, in fact as if I were the kind of person whose younger sister would join the CIA.

"... but still Zoe has to live with her conscience. After all, even if you insist on looking at the matter from a radical lesbian point of view—"

"That's exactly how I look at it," interrupted Bronwen. "I don't see any reason to apologize for being radical, and any other point of view is suicidal."

"Well, fine," I said. "I'm not arguing politics."

"But **I** am," said Bronwen. "Sex **is** politics."

"**Anyway,**" I said; this sort of argument about gender politics seemed much more exhausting than useful, since I did not anticipate either of us persuading the other, and Zoe did not seem in any condition to join in. "**Anyway,**" I went on, "even if you look at it from a radical point of view, it would be one thing to have **meant** to kill Gurney and feel morally correct about it as a battle won against sexism, but it's quite another matter to overreact and kill someone on the spur of the moment." I paused. "Personally, I find the latter more forgivable, but it takes a higher toll."

Bronwen still looked at me with disfavor, but no longer as though I were quite subhuman. "That may be," she said, "but you're totally ignoring real life. You know what'll happen if Zoe goes on trial. It's not just her life and career, it's also Lina's."

"I don't see why Lina has to be mentioned," I said. "Surely Zoe can confess without dragging Lina into it."

Both of them looked at me as though I had gone mad.

"Just how the hell do you propose that she do that?" demanded Bronwen. "If she goes to trial, the prosecutor'll interrogate her pretty damn specifically. She won't be able to get away with just mumbling that Gurney threatened her in some indeterminate way. Besides which, everybody knows Zoe's gay, and half of them know about Lina. Can you imagine what a fucking circus it'll be? Do you have any conception how nasty people will be even if Lina somehow stays out of it? Do you realize that life will be hell for Zoe from the minute she goes to the police, because she's a woman, a lesbian, and she killed a man?"

"Life already seems to be hell for her," I commented.

"Yes, **but.**"

"Well, why does it have to come out that she's gay?" I said. "She's not famous or anything."

Bronwen again looked at me as if I were something akin to a nasty grub found chewing up the lettuce. "Are you really this naïve, or are you just stupid?" she inquired. "These things always come out. Besides, it's always better to take the offensive. She has to let them know she's gay from the start. In this world you have to fight for everything—for your rights, for your beliefs, for your very existence." She stopped, having made a rhetorical error. "**You** don't," she corrected herself with a basilisk-like glare, "**we** do. **All** women do. And if Zoe goes to the police they'll grind her up like hamburger. At the very least she'll be locked up for years and reduced to a career of gay-rights prison activism."

I reflected that Bronwen might not be wrong. It was certainly not anything I wanted Zoe to go through. And yet ...

"I'll just have to do what I have to do," said Zoe.

"Which means?" said Bronwen.

Before Zoe could answer, there was another knock at the door and Renee entered.

"Sorry," she said, "I need to get some books."

"That's okay," said Zoe. "It doesn't make any difference. Nothing makes any difference. I killed Richard Gurney and it doesn't matter who knows it."

"Oh," said Renee. She stood there for a minute looking at us, then picked up the books on her desk and went very quietly out.

31

The Gang of Four were displeased. They were not sure that Zoe should have gone to the police. On the other hand, they disagreed totally with all of Bronwen's arguments, and labeled her a potential terrorist—except for Carolyn, who said that she at least saw what Bronwen was getting at, even if she didn't like it.

Their displeasure stemming primarily from the lack of a tidy solution to Richard Gurney's death, there was not much to be said to them, especially by me. They seemed to feel, quite unfairly, that I had hounded Zoe into a decision she might otherwise not have made. My pointing out that Bronwen had pressed Zoe towards the opposite decision for more than a week fell on unreceptive ears. They were determined that, no matter what Zoe had decided, they would have found it unsatisfactory.

In vain did I point out to them that in such a case there could be no happy ending; that even had the killer been a crazed and repellent sort, he or she would no doubt possess a sorrowing or at least deeply embarrassed relative who would be wounded by the matter. But they were not interested in this.

It occurred to me that they were jealous at my having realized the solution after reading their notes; but they denied this. They were not to be satisfied.

Malcolm was grieved, and wished that someone less appealing than Zoe had done it: someone less intelligent, less scrupulous, and less sensible. Evan was at first excited, and then angry; he found the whole business distasteful and felt that Zoe's having done it wronged him in some deep personal way—for he was fond of Zoe and now she had proved even more imperfect than Carolyn (he was, he confided to me, glad Carolyn had not learned any martial arts or Gurney would have been dead long ago). Liz was shocked, but put it out of her mind and wrote a paper on the Brontës that had to be retyped after Hemingway desecrated it; Kathy and Linda greeted me with "Keith, you nosy bastard, now look what you've done! No more hamster funerals for you, you hear?" and Dave and Myron were interested but philosophical. Somebody had to have done it, they indicated, and if it hadn't been one of my friends then I would probably not have guessed who.

"Damn, Keith," Mariah Sebastian kept saying as she nagged me again for printable details. "**Zoe Vogel!**" She looked confounded as she lolled in my desk chair on Tuesday afternoon, but her curiosity was unabated. "Our good pal Zoe! Jeez. I hate this. Tell me more."

We had all gone over the details of the murder and its solution: I had told of the sherry party and how Richard Gurney had then come to Zoe's room threatening to keep Lina Troyer from getting tenure; how Zoe had hit him in the throat and seen him die on her bedroom floor; how Bronwen had arrived without knocking and convinced her that they must stow him in the lounge so that he would be found without reference to them. How Renee, returning from class, had overheard enough of their conversation to suspect what had happened, and had decided to make the report herself; how Gilbert and Lainey had put the body in the trash and abandoned the blanket in the Quad on their way to a party. How first Dawnya and then we had discovered the body, and how Dawnya had said nothing but we had called the police and chosen to make our own inquiries.

"Keith, this is terrible," said Mariah. "How the hell am I supposed to write about Zoe killing him?"

"Well, don't write about it then," I said. "Who says you have to write about it?"

"You don't get it," said Mariah. "What kind of historian are you, anyway? This is big news. We gotta have it. Just because I like Zoe—but God, what a fucking mess. I swear I liked the serial killer idea better. Now Zoe'll end up in jail instead of grad school, and Lina'll not only definitely miss out on tenure but nobody else'll want to hire her. How totally fucked."

I looked out the window, watching people wander in and out of the College Office, and wondered when Mariah would cease to rave. "Are you implying that Zoe shouldn't have turned herself in?" I inquired.

"No, no, not at all," said Mariah hastily. "You were right. She was right. Killing people is wrong. You can't let people go around killing people, it'd tear up the fabric of society."

Briefly, I wondered who had originally come up with that nonsense about the fabric of society. It might once have meant something, but I did not think the world was so homogeneous. If there had ever been a fabric, it had long since been ripped to shreds and each shred had been eaten by a different breed of worm, or been put in a different religion's shrine to cover a different saint's decaying fingernails.

"Well, what are you going to do about this article?" I asked. "I already told Zoe she didn't need to drag Lina into it, and she thought I was crazy."

"She's right," said Mariah. "Even if we don't print anything tomorrow or next week—even if we decide to be bad journalists and sit on the story—it'll all come out sooner or later. It's like an old tampon: the bloody thing's got to come out sometime."

"Well, what are you going to do?" I repeated, recoiling from this repellent analogy. "Put in the details and leave out the names?"

"I could, I suppose," she said irresolutely. "Jesus, I hate ethical questions. Life's fucked enough without that. Shit, did I tell you there's a warrant out on me for not paying my goddamn car registration? Plus that I'm an uninsured motorist? Plus that I can't afford to get a new muffler? Do you realize that the cops're going to be chasing me all over town in that clunker and when they catch me they'll prob'ly put me away for as long as Zoe? Have you ever eaten that congealed fat they pass off as food at the county jail? I mean shit, life is crazy even without ethical whatsits." She sighed, then leaped up, knocking my nearly unknockable chair to the floor. "Jesus, I'm parked in a towaway zone!" she wailed. "How could I do that, the campus police'll impound it!"

She was off, leaving a pencil or two where there had been no pencils before, and I got off my bed, put them into my pencil jar, and began to read about the diminution of Romania during the early 1940s. Hitler hadn't been very protective of his disorganized eastern ally. Machiavelli would have applauded.

But the Gang of Four remained displeased, and wished for a more convenient solution. They sulked slightly, with Pauline working furiously on her canvas of Aunt Jemima and the Jolly Green Giant, Tricia worrying whether she should try to look like Siouxsie Sioux on a daily basis or somehow bleach her hair back to brown, and Holly and Carolyn orchestrating tech and dress rehearsals for their abominable play.

"If those actors don't toe the line tonight," Holly proclaimed frequently, "they'll have only themselves to blame if the audience throws fruit."

"Or rotten eggs," Carolyn would add dreamily.

Thus we went on for several days. Mariah wrote a brief, guarded article; Gilbert and Lainey reappeared without noticeable change and with a surprising lack of rancor ("Jail was a real drag," they were heard to remark, laughing; "wait'll they make us show up at the trial!"); and the Personals column of **Fun Times** hissed "Frodo, you blew it this time. No more kisses. Nogales."

"I wonder what that means?" said Tricia avidly.

"Cookbook Recipe Explodes When Followed," quoted Pauline in sibylline tones.

On Thursday afternoon Zoe's parents put up her bail and removed her from the pernicious influence of Lina, Bronwen, the History department, and the university in general; and on Thursday night Holly and Carolyn's show opened to a small but fruit-less audience.

On Friday morning, Pauline pronounced herself finished with Aunt Jemima and the Jolly Green Giant; on Friday afternoon Evan announced his desire to study Sociology; and Tricia had her hair bleached at the local beauty college.

At dinner Malcolm suggested we all see Holly and Carolyn's play, and after we and they had returned from this interesting fiasco (we had offered to throw eggs, but they had declined our proposal on janitorial grounds), Evan put on a Jefferson Airplane record, Holly brought out a bottle of tequila, and Tricia lobbed a spoonful of yams at me.

"How did you know it was Zoe?" asked Liz from the comfort of the phone alcove couch; apparently no one else wanted to know.

"It was obvious, really," I said, "obvious once I considered the evidence."

"But we saw all the same evidence as you did, didn't we?"

"Pretty much," I said. I did not mention Zoe's apparently innocuous note ("What do you know? I'm moving downtown!"); just because it had happened to prove a mental catalyst for me did not mean it would have been one for anyone else.

"I suppose we would have thought of it some-time," said Liz.

"There's no question of **that,**" said Holly. She put her arm around Carolyn and they clinked mugs. "We should never have given him our notes."

"Nope," said Carolyn gaily, "we should've eaten them." She began to sing in Old French, or was it Provençal?

> Douce dame jolie,
> Pour Dieu ne pense's mie

Que nulle ait signourie
Seur moy fors vous seulement.
Qu'a de's sans tricherie
Chierie
Vous ay et humblement
Tous les jeurs de ma vie
Servie
Sans vilein pensement.

The words did not seem to bear any relation to the situation, but perhaps I was merely being dense.

"I think," said Evan as we downed our second and third drinks, "that we should go and turn all the sculptures in the dining room to face the wall."

None of the sculptures in the dining room have faces, or even front or back, but it seemed like a good idea, especially since it involved climbing onto ledges some twenty feet off the ground.

Consequently, we greeted this proposal with great enthusiasm.

"Turn the sculptures!" chanted Tricia and Pauline.

"Turn the sculptures!" proclaimed Holly and Carolyn.

"Turn the sculptures!" grinned Malcolm and I.

"Turn the sculptures!" we all exclaimed in a monumental clinking of mugs and glasses.

Then we all put down our mugs and glasses and went off to the dining room to turn the sculptures. It was not quite the same as inurning hamsters, but it had the advantage of lacking Richard Gurney's corpse.

Perhaps life would return to normal after all.

ACKNOWLEDGEMENTS

Thanks are due to the many members of Berkeley's venerable Thursday's Child writers' group for their comments on the early chapters, and to Sedigitus Swift for comments and suggestions throughout.

About the Author

Colette Tajemna has been an avid mystery reader since the age of eight, when she was surprised to discover that mysteries, not mythology or fairy tales, constituted the largest category of oral book reports she had presented at school. Among her favorite mystery authors are (somewhat chronologically) Dorothy L. Sayers, Margery Allingham, Josephine Tey, Sarah Caudwell, Laurie R. King, Louise Penny, and (a more recent discovery) Richard Osman. She's also enjoyed many a book by (alphabetically) Lawrence Block, Christianna Brand, Raymond Chandler, Colin Cotterill, Amanda Cross, Martha Grimes, Gregory McDonald, Adrian McKinty, Ellis Peters, Elizabeth

Peters, Ruth Rendell, Georges Simenon ... and on and on!

She lives with two house rabbits, neither of which is named Hemingway.

Colette also writes as Karla Huebner. You may learn more about her books, and sign up for her newsletter, at www.karlahuebner.com.

ALSO FROM ARCHELAUS

The Tales from Ondiran series,
by Sedigitus Swift:

The Eye of Ksera
Sorceress for Hire
Sinta, Sorceress-Detective
The Misadventures of Thonir

www.ingramcontent.com/pod-product-compliance
Lightning Source LLC
Chambersburg PA
CBHW061333310726
48974CB00001B/25